Jo and her team successfully prevented the second invasion. Only a single enemy Scout made it to Earth, but the horror it brought makes people shiver. For Jo, it's clear — to get ahead of another attack, she must enter hostile territory, even if there is no chance for a return journey.

Exploration: Lioness Tracks II
Copyright © 2019 Valerie J. Long
ISBN: 978-1-4874-2421-3
Cover art by Carmen Waters

Published by eXtasy Books Inc or
Devine Destinies, an imprint of eXtasy Books Inc

Look for us online at:
www.eXtasybooks.com or www.devinedestinies.com

EXPLORATION: LIONESS TRACKS II
ZOE LIONHEART BOOK 22

BY

VALERIE J. LONG

DEDICATION

To all who dream of space

PART ONE—COMING HOME

CHAPTER ONE

A hand gently touched my shoulder. The fog around my mind slowly cleared. I felt a throbbing pain at the back of my head. The hit must have been severe to have caused such an effect on my reinforced skin. I wondered why my *Analogy* had not suppressed the effect.

— *Acute lack of resources.* —

Oh, right, yes. I had given my reserves to Sylvie. After a short stay in space, her survival was balancing on a knife's edge. The lack of oxygen, bubbles in the body, the vessels that burst from decompression, possible radiation damages, and burns from the grazing shot were a tough challenge — even for a nano-enhanced Mamba. Her protective suit hadn't been of much help due to the burns.

Compared to Sylvie's injuries, my headache was a minor problem.

My partner Achrotzyber wasn't well, either. He was in Dragon stasis, so he was out of action but not currently in danger.

Regarding the action, we won! With nothing but our two thirty-meters-long Barracudas, we shot a fifty-kilometer-diameter Jelly mothership and its three landers to shreds. Thus the new invasion was stopped. And the other Barracuda was shot to shreds, too. That was the situation, wasn't it?

I opened my eyes. Francine leaned over me with a worried look on her face. "Are you okay, Jo?"

"Yes. Only a headache. Nothing serious. Is everything okay outside?"

1

"Nothing is stirring outside in the debris. No shots, no stray radiation from fusion reactors, nothing. I turned *Mischief* around and adapted the vector, but didn't move closer. The Scouts are still ahead of us."

"Yes. How long was I passed out?"

"A few minutes. Can I get anything for you?"

"A hot chocolate would be fine."

"I'll get one." Francine turned toward the galley. "What about Sylvie?"

"I hope we can get her through. Right now, we can't do much. I gave her all I could spare."

"Is that why you passed out?"

"Yes."

"Will it help if we return to Earth sooner?"

"We need at least two days to return anyway. By then, either my healing nanos saved her or she's dead."

Francine fell mute.

When Francine returned with two cups of hot chocolate, I was already sitting in my pilot seat again. "Thanks."

"You're welcome." She sat down and stared at her main screen. It displayed our course and the slowly spreading wreckage ahead.

"I was scared as shit," she said.

"You didn't say anything."

"No. I thought you had enough to worry about and didn't need to rack your brain for my sake. You were so calm. I thought I should at least try to remain as cool."

"Cool?" I took a sip of my hot chocolate. "I was just too shocked to show any fear. I could only think about our battle plan. I blocked out everything else."

"You can do that?"

"You could say that I've practiced blocking out unpleasant thoughts."

Francine took a sip from her cup. After a while, she asked, "It's really over, isn't it?"

With a wipe of my finger, I produced a graphic display of the anomaly data. "Look. The overshoots are gone, so there's currently no other spaceship passing through the wormhole. The main oscillations are already fading. Eduardo's program grants the wormhole a few more hours at best before it collapses. I don't think more will come."

With further finger moves, I marked parts of the wreckage as targets and made them a priority. "So yes, in principle, it's over. Of course, we still have to clean up here so that the wreckage can't do harm. Then there's also a rack with eighty-one Scouts on its way toward Earth. But I don't think that a few unarmed Scouts with a handful of invaders can cause us serious trouble."

CHAPTER TWO

I returned to the cockpit with two cups of hot chocolate. I handed one to Francine and placed the other next to my seat.

"Sylvie's doing better. Her body accepted the nutrients from my nanos, and her healing is now making good progress. By the time we arrive, she should be able to stand."

"What about Arko?"

"He'll be okay soon, too. I don't want to wake him up before the burns are healed."

"Good."

After a glance at the screen, I sat down again. "The next reply should arrive soon. I'm curious how Zoé fared against the Scouts."

"Cumbersome," Francine said. "Oh, sorry, I meant the communication, not Zoé."

"Yes." A true dialogue wasn't possible across these distances. We delivered our report to Earth after we had destroyed all parts of the wreckage and directed the smaller parts toward the Sun. Now we just had to wait for a reply from Earth. Meanwhile, there was plenty of time to look after the injured and prepare a cup of hot chocolate or two.

Sometime later, Jeff Scott, the Australian Minister for Defence, appeared on our screens. In the background, I recognized rows of computer tables and diligent people in uniform.

"Black One, this is Jeff Scott speaking from the Asia-Pacific War Room. Congratulations on your victory and my best wishes for your injured comrades' fast recovery. Humanity owes you infinitely much. That's more clear to us today than ever before. Francine Besson, Sylvie Moreau, Johanna Meier, Achrotzyber Paxxchfztnach, your readiness to sacrifice yourselves puts us with our petty political struggles to shame."

That went down like the hot chocolate. Francine shuffled in her seat at the mention of her name. Was he only talking to us? Or was this conversation being broadcast live? Obviously, he had practiced my partner's name.

"At this point, I expressly want to highlight the performance of our dauntless fighter pilot Zoé Lionceau. She intercepted and destroyed a large part of the enemy Scouts behind the moon with her bold venture into space. Overall, she scored eighty kills."

"Zoé?" Francine called out.

I only nodded. If Zoé went behind the moon, that meant she maxed out the Taipan's technical features. Its technology could provide the pilot with oxygen for hours and could protect her against radiation, overheating, and hypothermia. However, there was no food, drink, or a toilet to use while she was flying. Plus she could only find her way back if she could still see our planet.

"You don't have to worry once you've come back. Your teammate already cleaned everything up." Jeff smiled through the screen. "I've been talking long enough. We're expecting you in eight and a half hours in Gladstone. I personally want to shake hands with you. War room, over."

His picture froze. Francine and I looked at each other.

"What does that mean?" she asked.

"That we should take a nap and a shower beforehand. That sounds like a party to me."

CHAPTER THREE

Our home's blue-and-white water and cloud pattern slowly grew beyond the screen's edges. The outskirts of individual continents became visible, and Australia moved into the picture on the left side of the screen.

"Marvelous!" Sylvie's voice sounded weak but happy. For the first time in four days, she had cautiously left her sick bed and sat down in my pilot seat.

I noticed Achrotzyber watching Sylvie closely. "Do you feel the same as her about seeing Earth, Companion?"

"I'm not sure. How should I feel, Companion?" my partner asked. He held on to the handles at the rear cockpit bulkhead next to me.

"Well—comforted, I'd say."

"What is the reason for this feeling?"

"It's our home world," Francine explained from her seat.

"It must be because we regard the familiar colors as reassuring," I added. "Space is hostile. The sight of our planet subliminally signals a place of survival in this environment."

"Ah. I understand."

Perhaps I spoke nonsense, but as long as the reply sounded plausible to my Dragon Companion, I was happy with it, too. Now I'd enjoy my return. The sight of Earth—even if it was only via screen—had to help us all to digest the past battle's horrors.

I'd have preferred to simply snuggle into my partner's strong arms and let him hold me tight until the events were only a faded memory, but our overcrowded Barracuda wasn't the right place for that.

The computer steered us in the direction of the eastern Australian coast and smoothly decelerated. At the elevation of five-hundred kilometers, it activated our transponder and thus announced our touchdown.

Shortly, we received the first signal.

"War Room Asia-Pacific. Welcome back, Black One. We'll hand you over to Gladstone."

We soon heard the familiar voice of our local chief flight controller. "Black One for Gladstone. Welcome back and a happy new year!"

Francine briefly checked our radio's status and saw that the microphone at her seat was active. "Gladstone for Black One, thank you very much. We ask for touchdown clearance."

"Black One, you're cleared for touchdown on the main run-way. Your landing space is marked. I'm pretty sure you can't miss it."

"Gladstone, do I understand right that we shall land on the airport?"

"Correct. A few people are waiting to welcome you."

"We feared something like that."

"Come on, that's part of it. Don't worry. Your people have got everything under control."

Francine turned to me. I only winked at her.

She nodded and gazed ahead again. "Gladstone, we're looking forward to you. As long as the beer's cold and the men are hot enough, we'll be happy."

CHAPTER FOUR

"Good morning, guys and gals, in Australia and all over the world. It's Saturday, the first of January 2067. I'm Pop Verne of ABC Queensland. We're greeting you from Gladstone airport, where in a few minutes our victorious space fighters will land. On this marvelous summer day, we've prepared a big show for you. So stay tuned, and we'll get the party started!"

The screen flashed to a graphical display of our approach to the left and a picture of the sky above Gladstone to the right.

I switched my main screen and zoomed our cameras on Gladstone. The airport wasn't hard to find, but the hot air above the city didn't allow for an entirely sharp picture.

The largest part of the airfield was teeming with people. There was only one free space, marked by a fifty-meter long red cross.

"We indeed can't miss our landing space," I noted. "If someone had it in for us, that would be the ideal place to hit us. So let's hope the bad guys prefer to celebrate with us today."

Francine gave me an irritated glance.

"Sorry. I don't want to spoil it for any of you, but please be at least a bit alert at the beginning. Yes? Also, please keep the suits on while you're in public."

"Jo, we're *Mambas*," Sylvie reminded me reproachfully. "We know how to act in large crowds."

"You're right, sorry. Okay. Hopefully, the speeches won't take too long."

"Hopefully there aren't too many speakers," Francine said. "Do you think we can have something to drink before?"

"Depends on who's sponsoring the party." I pointed at a group of waving pennants. "If I have the colors right, they'll make every effort to provide us with a bottle of bright golden barley brew in front of the photographers."

A faint ringing reminded us that the autopilot had reached its programmed endpoint, about three-thousand meters above the city. Francine and I glanced at each other. I nodded at her and pointed at her data glove.

So Francine dealt with the touchdown maneuver of our spaceship. With a shove, she changed our downward direction so that our vector pointed exactly to the center of the large red cross. During the descent, she reduced the speed of our ship until we gently sailed down toward the ground.

"I only have one problem," she admitted. "Which way should the bow point?"

"Align with the Taipan."

"Oh, sure."

A single woman in her protective suit stood in front of the slender fighter's tip and gazed up at us—Zoé.

"Cool girl," Sylvie judged.

"And she was all alone," Francine added. Then she focused on her virtual flight stick and carefully placed our space fighter down at the center of the cross.

"Thanks, Francine. Now, out with you."

"You go first," Sylvie objected.

"I don't mind."

CHAPTER FIVE

I took a deep breath as the hatch swung open and the ladder unfolded toward the ground. The air smelled like a mix of burned aviation fuel, hot asphalt, dry dust, sweat, a hint of fried meat, and salty ocean. What a difference from the filtered and recycled air aboard our spacecraft!

The silence engulfing me formed a strong contrast to the aromas surrounding us. Were the people no longer there? But yes, naturally, only they weren't moving.

Zoé looked up at me expectantly from her place in front of the Taipan. I ignored the ladder and jumped down to the airfield, and then I turned around and watched Sylvie climb down the first rungs. She trembled a little but managed to come down to me without aid, then proudly assumed her position beside me.

Francine and Achrotzyber had no problems with the ladder, either.

As soon as we all had left the ship, Zoé walked up to us.

"Come with me," she said.

Before Zoé could turn around though, Francine hugged her. "Hearty congratulations, *sister.*"

Zoé tried to protest, but found herself in Sylvie's arms, next. "Great job, lioness!" Sylvie praised.

Zoé smiled and briefly allowed me and Achrotzyber to hug her as well. "So, now we must go. We'll have plenty of time for hugs later."

"Do you know the agenda?"

"Only the beginning. Come with me to the markings

there."

She led us to a group of five chalk markings. The letters Z, F, J, A, and S were written on the asphalt and showed what was expected from us. There were little microphones stuck to the ground, too. I gave Francine and Sylvie a meaningful glance and briefly analyzed the overall picture my *Analogy* recorded. I didn't find any indications of a sniper rifle. I didn't sense disruptor fields nearby, either. I did sense the stray emissions of micro fusion generators like the ones our armor suits used. They guarded the airport's outskirts.

As soon as we had assumed our positions, a trumpet behind us blared. Drums and bagpipes chimed in. Then cheers and applause rolled over us.

While we were distracted by the noise, a delegation of four people dared to advance, accompanied by two camera teams. I recognized the Australian Prime Minister, our retired Air Force Marshal Jenny, and Tess, the head of my secret security team. I didn't recognize the fourth person's face, but based on his attire — namely his headscarf with golden headbands — he looked very Arabic.

As he didn't care about Tess' figure-hugging combat suit, he'd tolerate our skintight space suits as well. It was too late to change outfits now. Four meters away from us, the group stopped at another set of chalk markings. The camera people went to both sides of our lines, each team targeting one line. Now we had to wait until the music and storm of excitement calmed down.

I was still wondering whether the Prime Minister or the stranger would approach us first due to protocol when Tess approached me.

"Legata Aurea Victoria Johanna, welcome back to Earth. On behalf of the Dragon University and all *Protectors* on Earth, I congratulate all of you for your victory."

The address *Legata Aurea* was obvious. Yes, I was a Golden

Dragon, a *Protector,* and I had formally accepted being the former Dragon empress' legate. But *Victoria?*

My Dragon *memory* provided me with an image of the first *victorious* Dragon legate who had destroyed an extraterrestrial invader's spaceship. She, Elaine Lionheart, had been the first legate carrying that title. In which case I probably had to live with it, too.

"Thank you, Tess." I reached out a hand.

Tess ignored the offered hand. Instead, she wrapped me tightly into her arms. "Gee, Jo, good that nothing happened to you. We were so scared for you. When the one Barracuda's grav field emissions suddenly ceased, nobody dared to say a word."

One by one, she hugged the others, too. After, she returned to her mark and nodded at Jenny. Why Jenny?

Jenny took a step forward. "Paladin Johanna, on behalf of the Order of the Dying Lioness, I heed you welcome back. Well done!" She nodded at my female teammates. "The Order formally received and approved the nominations for Sylvie Moreau, Francine Besson, and Zoé Lionceau as Knights of the Order. Paladin Johanna, I herewith forward these nominations to you."

Oh. I nodded. So Jenny represented the Order today. That was why she addressed me as Paladin. Of course, as Legata Aurea, I had the last say. "I agree with the nominations."

"Then I may tell you that our schedule for today leaves time for a ceremony."

That was pragmatically prepared like a Dragon would have handled it. "Well organized," I praised. "Thank you, Knight Jenny."

"I thank you for your confidence in me — in us all. Thank you that we were allowed to help you. Thank you for guiding us. Without you, the Jellies would have caught us with our pants down."

"Or without pants at all," I quietly murmured.

Jenny smirked and turned to her side. "May I introduce you both? Jo, this is Sheikh Rashid bin Khalifa Al Maktoum from Dubai, recently appointed United Nations Secretary for Interstellar Defence. He will be the administrative commandant of the UN armor suits, the UN Taipans, and — once we have any — the UN Barracudas. Sheikh Rashid, the Legata Aurea Johanna Meier, military commandant of Earth's defenses."

The Sheikh stepped forward and shook my hand. "It's an honor for me to meet you. Your dedication to Earth's survival puts us to shame and — at the same time — encourages us. I bow before your greatness."

Which he then did indeed.

"I'm glad to meet you. To be honest, I must admit that I didn't know before my departure that there was such a position in the UN."

"I took office five days ago. We had to make a quick decision, as it wasn't clear whether you'd be successful. Now it seems as if I could put this office to rest." He smiled in a friendly way.

"I hope that very much." I could have told him that this attacker didn't belong to the announced second wave, but had arrived somehow out-of-bands — but I didn't want to spoil my mates' party. "We should have a private talk within a couple of days."

"I'm very interested in visiting your University."

"Oh."

Rashid's face expressed how worried he was about my reaction. I quickly put up another smile. "You're welcome, of course. I just thought of our dress code on the island."

"Oh." He blushed slightly. "Yes, I've heard of that. Perhaps you should visit my country someday."

"I'd gladly visit Dubai again. It's nice there." Despite my

comment, I recalled being forced to participate in a Cartel execution in Dubai. Those times were over now, though.

Percy was rocking back and forth with a little unrest. I decided not to extend the conversation with Rashid any further and show some mercy on the Prime minister. Still, I took some time to introduce Sheikh Rashid to my comrades-in-arms.

He repeated each one's name and thanked them for their dedicated participation. Then he made way for the Australian Prime Minister.

What kind of speech had Percy prepared?

But the head of state simply came to me, bent his knees and wrapped both arms around me and lifted me up—with a wheeze. Due to my nanos, I was a bit heavier than appropriate for my height.

Needless to say, he put me back down rather quickly. "Thank you, Jo. Thanks for everything. Welcome back." He made a step back to nod at my comrades. "Thank you all. I had prepared a little speech. But there are no words to describe what you've done for us, so I only say once again—thank you. Happy new year, welcome back to Earth, and welcome to the party."

"Everyone has been mentioning this party," I replied. "What else is on the agenda, and is there anything to drink?"

"Sure, Jo." He clapped his hands. Nine children started from the free space's boundaries and hurried toward us with large, full glasses of beer. "After this, Liza will perform a concert. Around noon, we'll have the award ceremony, then a little press conference. After that, there will be a large barbie. The Gladstone Groovers will play there. From the late afternoon onward, we'll have rock bands on two stages."

He enumerated a list of prominent names that, like this *Liza*, sounded distantly familiar to me, then finally paused when he noticed my expression. "You don't know them all?"

"I guess I do. I've heard those names before."

"The greatest stars of the last decade and you only heard about them?"

"I haven't had much time for culture lately."

He fell silent at that, embarrassed.

CHAPTER SIX

Zoé, Francine, and Sylvie wore their new brooches with a lot of pride. The pin was of a silver lioness with a broken hind leg. Its body was speared, and its paw was raised to strike. It was ten centimeters wide and went well with undecorated black protective suits. My brooch was crimson metallic and less eye-catching.

The three women looked like inseparable friends. There wasn't any hint of the separation Zoé had struggled with at the beginning. Like a pack of lionesses, they were on the hunt for men.

Without their decorations as Knights of the Order of the Dying Lioness, men would have lined up to meet them. But not many confident suitors dared to address the war heroines. Those brave enough to talk to the women only wanted an interview. Our Mambas were systematically trained to keep their mouths shut when talking to the press, though.

I didn't have much time to watch the three women or even copy them. I was just glad that several young men in the sponsor's colorful uniforms catered to me. They provided me with drinks and brought me a steak from the barbecue on request, while I entertained all the people approaching me. There were many people—aside from the Prime Minister and the Secretary—who wanted to congratulate me in person and exchange a few words with me, including ambassadors, soldiers, lobbyists, scientists, the list seemed never-ending.

"Hello, Mikhail," I greeted the familiar face of the Russian space scientist whose research I had once *borrowed* without his consent. "Did the travel approval finally work?"

"Thanks, yes. Sadly much too late to be of use for you."

"That will turn out, Mikhail. This time, we were only out there for a few days. We have no elaborate concepts for a longer stay in space yet."

"What are you thinking of?"

"I'd say, if we want to make it hard for the Jellies, we should have resupply bases for our space fighters in the asteroid belt or on Saturn's moons. Perhaps it would make sense to relocate the production lines for our space fighters out there, in case the Jellies show up with a whole fleet."

Mikhail frowned. "I thought you already defeated the second wave?"

I changed to Russian. "Mikhail, that attack was irregular and not the second wave. But we should talk about that later, on the island. Today's for celebrating."

After that, I gave him a kiss on the cheek and turned to the next congratulator, an elegantly dressed young lady.

"Buon giorno," she greeted me shyly. When I spotted Marcello — the Minister of Defense in Italy — and his spouse in the back, I recognized my Italian girlfriend. I was glad we were meeting each other again under better circumstances, unlike the day I had prevented her kidnapping.

"Buon giorno. You've grown up a lot!" I winked at her and waved her parents close. "How are you doing? Come, I'll introduce you to my Companion."

CHAPTER SEVEN

A rock concert was new for me. As a child, I hadn't had money to buy a ticket for one. Later, I was too busy with my job and my side jobs. Since I joined the world savior business, there was little time for such extravagancies.

At least the loud music gave me an excuse to just snuggle into Achrotzyber's arms for a while, instead of explaining to the hundred-and-first lobbyist that I made my purchases the way I wanted and had no interest in bid processes. The tall man at my side also discouraged any admirers from approaching me. It was clear to any potential suitors that they couldn't compete with my Companion. On the other hand, young girls didn't approach my partner once they spotted the red brooch over my left breast.

Our three girls had meanwhile disappeared. I hoped they had their fun, at least. They certainly deserved it.

What is this enormous unfolding of noise good for, Companion?

For entertainment. For distraction or for inspiring the imagination. It's not productive activity but satisfies the emotional needs of illogical creatures. Don't you like it?

I could perchance try to analyze the emotion-influencing components within the complex vibration patterns. If only their creators were not so imprecise in their performance.

Imprecise?

There is a fundamental rhythm, which the man with the instrument with the six metal strings never really meets.

You mean, the lead guitar plays out of beat?

That is a fact, not an opinion.

18

Okay. Well, this isn't about mathematical precision.
But?
If you can't appreciate the music, just watch the audience.
I didn't have this option. Except for the shoulder blades of the people before me, there wasn't much to watch.

PART TWO—VISITORS

CHAPTER EIGHT

Tess is on her way to us, Companion.

Swiftly, and with grim determination, our Mamba leader made her way through the crowd. At first, I only spotted the heads of people making way for her. Then she stood before me. "Jo, come quick."

"What's up?"

"Problems." She turned around and pushed her way through the spectators again. I followed her, and my Companion assumed the rear.

Tess led us to the terminal building. She brought us to a side room, where Percy, Rashid, Jenny, Rod, and an unknown soldier with captain's insignia were already waiting for us.

Zoé, Sylvie, and Francine followed close behind us. I assumed they realized something was going on.

Percy gave the Sheikh a short glance. Then he nodded toward the captain. "Captain Becker, please report."

"Okay." He nodded toward Achrotzyber and me. "Legata, Protector, we received a distress call from the salvage team assigned to the crashed enemy Scout. We had deployed an entire company of paratroopers, but lost contact after receiving the call. Now, nobody's answering. That's the status as of half an hour ago. The War Room sent out two reconnaissance planes right away. We should soon receive the first pictures. But first, the last message."

He fetched a tablet computer, tapped on it, and showed us the screen with a video image of a lot of red sand, a roughly drop-shaped mountain of metal, and a few soldiers in camouflage suits.

"*We have contact now. The Scout looks quite damaged. It will surely never fly again. I don't see Jellies. The Major lets us circle the Scout. Here – there are two guys already. How did they get here?*" Shots were fired. "*Damn, they're fast!*"

The image blurred, and the video ended.

"What was the brown stuff spraying around there?" Francine asked.

"The two strangers tossed parts of their body substance toward the soldiers," Achrotzyber said. That matched my observation. "The bullets were without effect. They simply passed through the body. Despite the humanoid shape, these cannot be normal human beings."

"No," I agreed and looked at the Prime Minister.

"We need your help, Jo. We're facing a strange enemy, and I fear our soldiers can't handle such aliens. We've alerted further units, but how shall we fight this enemy?"

CHAPTER NINE

Somewhat clueless, I stared at the screen. I figured we weren't dealing with the second wave, but I hadn't expected such a turn of events.

Do you have an idea, Companion?

Yes.

Speak up.

Achrotzyber addressed the captain. "Where exactly did the Scout land?"

"In the Simpson Desert, about four hundred kilometers southeast of Alice Springs."

"Then this area can be easily cordoned off. I recommend installing a quarantine zone."

"Well, yes." The captain gazed helplessly at the Prime Minister.

"The Legata Aurea's Companion commands," I firmly corrected. "On behalf of all Protectors, I accept the Australian Government's request for assistance and assume supreme command. Install an outer perimeter along the main roads that surround the desert and prepare everything to add an inner quarantine ring of perhaps fifty kilometers in diameter. We'll control the quarantine from the air."

I turned toward my companion. "Achrotzyber, what else?"

"As the extraterrestrial life form can separate parts of its body mass, we must postulate a variable shape," my Companion explained. "If this creature is not bound to a human shape, animals must be prevented from leaving the quarantine zone, too. Nobody should come closer than twenty meters to a potentially infected person. For fighting it over distance, I recommend plasma weapons. For close-range fights, I recommend flame throwers. Once we know how to recognize an infected person, we can consider decontamination procedures."

"How can you safely contain such an area?" the Sheikh asked.

"With disruptor fields," I quickly decided.

I turned to my lead *Mamba*. "Tess, we need all the spare equipment available on the island or at the factory for such fields."

"Jenny, have the Order publish an inquiry to the unknown terrorist group that we need every single grav field projector they're hiding anywhere, in exchange for no matter what."

Both women nodded.

As we had a new official, I asked him for assistance as well. "Mr. Secretary, we'll need your help with a logistic challenge we're facing. We must find a way to carry equipment here from every part of Earth as fast as possible, if necessary, on a supersonic fighter's co-pilot seat."

Rashid nodded, and I went on, "If fire helps us, we'll need fuel. We might need to incinerate a larger area, so you should look for firebombs. In the worst case, we might need to deploy a tactical nuclear bomb."

"What are you thinking of?" Percy asked, aghast.

"Obviously, these aren't stones, but if these creatures spread as fast as the Monolith Monsters, we've got no time to waste. Mighty, let's take the Barracuda."

Percy didn't seem to understand my reference about the Monolith Monsters. My predecessor had left me her memory of a black-and-white movie from 1957, where extraterrestrial stone blocks had spread like a plague. Somehow, that memory had just come up.

I only feared that salt water wouldn't do for us this time.

"What about us?" Francine asked.

"Come along. When the two of us exit, the fighter still needs pilots. Zoé, your Taipan is still configured with plasma cannons, isn't it?"

"Yes."

"You'll give us cover, then."

"Okay."

CHAPTER TEN

I felt a bit sorry for the party guests, but it was impossible to start the Barracuda and the Taipan without being noticed. My Companion encoded the destination coordinates into the computer, then made room for Francine on her pilot seat. Meanwhile, I gently pushed Sylvie toward my seat.

"It will probably go as always," I commented. "I start on a reconnaissance mission and end up in the heart of the action—and as always, I don't have a plan yet. How do you engage an opponent throwing brown lumps around?"

"Stay out of reach. Avoid getting hit," Sylvie proposed, probably quoting Mamba lessons. "Even better would be staying out of sight."

"We're on our way," Francine said and turned away from her dashboard. "When facing enemy forces with unknown strength and combat is inevitable, our lessons say strike hard, and eliminate recognized targets with the highest possible effectiveness."

"If we follow that logic, a nuke would be safest," I concluded gloomily. "Actually, I want to avoid that."

"Once we reveal our presence, we must strike," Francine said. "Before the enemy can prepare for it."

"I thought I should have a look around first," I objected. "As long as we remain disguised, we're not forced to act."

"Companion," Achrotzyber began.

"I know, Mighty. That never works long for me, at least since we met. But did I ever tell you about my visit to the *Flying Gardens* hotel in Vegas? In, out, and far away with my loot before anyone even noticed it missing?"

Vegas was the first thought that came to my mind after leaving our Barracuda and entering the desert. It had been hot there, too, but not *that* hot.

In Las Vegas one usually took an air-conditioned car from one air-conditioned casino to the next, if one didn't consciously seek out the Inferno's sinful heat. I had ventured out to steal a radar device — not to hunt down an otherworldly organism with entirely unknown abilities, like today. Back then, Cartel killers had been after me. Those people carried knives and guns and bled like anyone else, unlike the enemies I was about to face.

However, like the killers in Las Vegas, the aliens didn't know that Velvet was already on their heels. Like the killers in Las Vegas, the aliens didn't know that Velvet could become invisible.

I didn't have a Dragon at my command in Vegas either, like I did now. Plus, these creatures had no place to hide from me, unlike the killers in the City of Sin.

Of course, this was all based on the information we'd received from the Captain. The reconnaissance planes hadn't delivered useful pictures yet.

This is close enough, I told Achrotzyber and stopped.

Five hundred meters away, the cooled-down wreckage of a crashed Jelly Scout stuck out of the sand. The end with the engine looked more or less intact — the grav field probably worked long enough to prevent the small spaceship from burning up.

Zoé didn't have to reproach herself. Eighty kills was a fantastic result. From a strategic point of view, her decision to let one Scout pass with a grazing hit to hunt other, intact invaders was entirely correct.

Two hundred meters ahead of me, several army vehicles

were parking. Soldiers were lying in the sand around them. At first, I couldn't tell where the reporter had sent his last message. Other than from the air, the encircling ring was no longer recognizable.

Nothing stirred in there. The area was too dry even for small lizards.

We must be grateful toward the invaders. In a rain forest area, they could have hidden better.

Surely, Companion. How will you gather new findings now?

I'll send out a nano probe.

For that, I squatted and placed one hand on the sand.

The thread of nano agents taken from the supplies inside my body quickly grew toward one of the lifeless bodies. From about two meters distance, I let my tiny extra eye collect new imagery.

No signs of life. From this perspective, I don't see injuries. Nor is there any sign of decay.

We do not know the foreign biochemistry, Companion. It can be lethal upon contact and still prevent decomposition.

There's no foreign biochemical sign of life either.

The foreign life form is in a strategically indefensible situation on hostile territory. It has good reasons not to show signs of life.

What would you do?

I am not in this situation.

Ask Francine and Sylvie.

It would take my Companion a while to describe the situation and ask them for their input. Meanwhile, I prepared another nano thread. A small healing nano column should suffice to examine one of the potentially contaminated bodies.

This nano column encountered unexpected resistance about one and a half meter before the body. It reported contact with an organic substance. The nano eye on my other thread confirmed a small brown spot that I had failed to notice before.

Then I lost contact with the healing nano column before it

could analyze the brown substance for me, and my nano eye reported the growth of the brown spot.

The signals in my second nano thread became distorted. I quickly got a confirmation for the only logical conclusion—the brown substance fed on nanos, and this feeding grew rapidly along the thread toward me.

I let both threads tear off my fingers, rose, and took several steps backward. With my enhanced bare eye, I could see the ground along the thread turn brown.

Crap!

Folks, the brown substance feeds on nanos.

I couldn't report more before three of the closest soldier bodies jumped up and stormed my way.

Jelly squitters!

CHAPTER ELEVEN

I had to change my location quick. It was all too clear that the nano threads gave their origin away. Sadly, my quick evasion maneuver didn't yield the desired result. The soldier bodies changed their direction, too. Why?

My camouflage should be good enough, and I wasn't any hotter than my surroundings, either. If it wasn't that, these beasts either noticed the draft of my movements or my footprints in the sand.

I suppressed the next curse and ran off. The creatures were running now, too, and they weren't any slower. Then I recognized — with the aid of the nano receptors in the back of my head — how one of the creatures swung back and tossed a brown lump toward me from full sprint.

I doubled backward and the lump missed.

Sadly, my change of course allowed my pursuers to close in on me. Next, the lump exploded and sent brown matter in all directions.

With a giant leap forward, I escaped the rain of strange substance. At the same time I recognized how all three pursuers swung back. If they placed their pseudo grenades skillfully, I'd be unable to evade them.

Faster. A sprint on the second Dragon power level significantly increased my head start — in exchange, I saw how *six* lumps flew in gigantic arcs, much farther forward than I had estimated. They placed mines along my potential escape routes.

Oh well, you asked for it. I stopped and turned around.

Recall nano skin. The camouflage no longer helped me. Plus, I shouldn't offer power food to the strange organisms. *Give me organic scales.*

– Two minutes. –

Two minutes without camouflage, without armor, without an option for escape. The enemies closed up fast, throwing more projectiles already at their . . . arms. No, not arms. They only had arm stumps left.

A plasma salvo from Zoé's onboard cannons blew up two of the three creatures. Now I knew for sure that the substance couldn't withstand this heat. I had hoped for that.

Sadly, a few plasma balls didn't suffice to fry it all. The un-burned remainders of the hit bodies were still active and now reformed to large piles that looked like dropped lumps, ready to burst.

My evil grin was probably lost on the aliens. My next ex-pression couldn't be mistaken, though. A lengthy burst of fire from my mouth burned the bodies and the remaining lumps to ashes.

Done.

Companion, that is not correct. You still face opposition, and you are surrounded.

Yes, now I recognized it, too. An entire company of pseudo soldiers came running toward me from the wreck. On top of that, where the thrown lumps had landed, bursting brown bubbles were distributing more and more blots on the desert sand.

You see that, too? The life form can spread out enormously fast.

You should withdraw.

Agreed. However, I'm only left with the third dimension to with-draw to – up.

A thought should suffice to spread my wings.

– The wing substance had to be used to form scales. –

We'll talk about that later.

Next, I told my Companion *I need a double plasma curtain toward the exit. Tell Zoé to target me, only with tenfold distance.*

I understand.

The creatures in the shape of assimilated soldiers were approaching fast. I had no time left.

Meanwhile, Zoé turned her Taipan around, returned, and fired as ordered. I triggered the third level and ran between the double salvo projectiles that made the desert floor blaze and the air boil. Zoé's shots scorched any brown substance along its path, incinerated my hair, and blistered my skin.

Thanks. Enough, I signaled once we had left the danger zone two kilometers behind.

It is not enough, my Companion disagreed.

Zoé turned around again and now targeted the individual pseudo bodies which were still following me.

The pain of the burns was about to make me pass out. *Heal.*

It was inevitable that the healing nanos had to return to the surface. I could only hope that I was far enough away from the brown goop.

Pick me up.

Negative. We may not risk contaminating the Barracuda.

What the —

No, of course, he was right. As long as we weren't sure I was truly clean, he couldn't take that risk. However, as I had to heal my skin to survive, this question would soon be answered.

CHAPTER TWELVE

The creature's bubble activities have stopped.
Thanks, Mighty. That was ultimately owed to the fact that Zoé turned any spot of the desert where anything stirred into a glass surface with her plasma cannons. *My thanks to Zoé.*

She only did what was logical.

Thank her. She's no expert in Dragon logic.

As you wish.

I patiently waited for my Companion to report back.

Zoé asked me to relay she only did what was necessary.

Of course. I looked up and waved at my comrades. Their camouflage was good, but their nestle field emission naturally told me where my teammates were hovering. *Now tell me what ideas Francine and Sylvie had before it started.*

Initially, Francine had said that in the situation it would be crucial for the enemy to stay under cover and grab a favorable opportunity to expand the mission base. Her analysis was confirmed as the battle continued. Sylvie recommends taking large-scale countermeasures now. What is your decision?

Dragon fire, as well as plasma bullets, are effective. So I deem the nuclear option disproportionate. I favor treating a wide range with firebombs. Then we can examine the area with nanos.

Nanos are endangered.

Exactly. The foreign organism seems unable to resist nanos, so we'll use it as bait. If there's indeed a remainder of the substance, it will become active. It shouldn't be difficult to reprogram decontamination nanos accordingly. I don't have to send out my own substance for that. Oh, and yes, if I'm still not considered clean, at least drop me some food and drink and a shade from the sun.

PART THREE—CONSULTATIONS

Chapter Thirteen

Someone approached me with energetic paces. I didn't take my gaze away from the flames.

"Legata Aurea?"

"Hello, Captain Becker. You needn't hurry. It's over."

"Sure?"

"If the flames are as hot as plasma fire, yes. The first attempt was a disaster."

"In what way?"

"The fire wasn't hot enough. The brown stuff resisted it. Individual particles rose with the smoke and continued to spread. That's why we had to burn a significantly larger zone now."

"Are you sure we made the perimeter wide enough?"

"Yes. We stopped the smoke spread in time." The first attempt with Dragon fire had cost Achrotzyber and me a lot of power. Before we could expend ourselves, my Companion had decided to spray his Wyvern poison, which proved to be a breakthrough success. Using poison was quite taxing on us, too. Neither of us could keep it up for long. Eventually, we ordered the deployment of special firebombs.

"Okay. And you've been sitting here for the last three days to watch the area of action?"

"Exactly."

"I don't have that much patience, Legata."

"Simply Jo."

"Jo. Well, okay, my name's Gus. Well, actually Gustav, but my friends call me Gus."

"Gus. Okay. Why are you here?"

"You requested a decontamination unit and a guard detachment. I was appointed to lead the guard detachment because we already know each other. At least that's what the General said."

"Because we already know each other."

"He said, that would be a Dragon thing."

There I had to grin, although he couldn't see it. "Okay, Gus. It's like with the firefighters. You're sure the fire's extinguished, but there's still a fireguard, in the unlikely case we've missed something. Achrotzyber developed a protocol that should rule out any danger to your unit. The very first thing you should do is examine and decontaminate me."

"Examine you?"

Was he blushing now? My nanos had already repaired my burned skin and now protected me against sunburn, but otherwise, I was nude. "Be painstakingly thorough."

CHAPTER FOURTEEN

I rose in one fluid motion and stood before the captain. "Gus, sorry, that was a joke. I'm a hundred percent clean. I've checked every bit of myself. I've also checked the burnt-down places. All places checked that way were clean, too. There were at most fragments of the organic substances. If it wasn't so, I wouldn't leave you alone with this plague. I need your help because I can't examine everything everywhere, the area is simply too large for that."

"I understand," he uttered with relief. Relief because he didn't have to examine me, or because he didn't have to fear the brown pest? "The Sheikh told me he urgently needs to talk to you once the situation allows it."

"Okay. Where is he? Still in Gladstone?"

"In Brisbane. He said he needed more infrastructure than Gladstone can offer for his UN contacts."

"Well. It's not every day that there's a party on the runway."

"No. But the international flights can't be handled there, not to mention the space a large plane needs. In any case he said you should just call and he'd cancel all other appointments."

"Then it has to be really important. I'll go to him next. Do you need anything else from me?"

"No."

"Sure?"

"Sure as one can be. If anything goes wrong here, I'll call. Until then I'll do fine on my own. The General clearly told me

I shouldn't bother you with my trifles. In exchange, I may call him directly. Shall I get you a helicopter?"

"Thanks, Gus, but I'll take my Barracuda. The Sheikh is already waiting for me."

"Oh, of course. Then I wish you a good journey."

"Thanks, Gus. Hold the fort, and remember the fireguard. We're relying on you."

"Of course, Jo. We have an idea now how sneaky that stuff can be. If we find an unburned spot anywhere, we'll burn it and check afterward." He added, "We're in Australia. You have to assume everything you don't know is poisonous."

"Nice motto. That's why they sent me someone who already knows me, right?"

He grinned. "Of all poisonous creatures in Australia, you're the most dangerous. No, not just here but in the entire world."

I laughed and patted his shoulder. "You're okay, Gus. We'll meet again."

"Yes, we will."

Francine took her feet off the control board when I entered the Barracuda. "Hello, Jo. Are we leaving?"

"Hello, Francine. The Sheikh is waiting for us in Brisbane."

"Brisbane is it? I haven't been there before." She gave me a mischievous smile.

I smiled back. "You can come along." Then I pointed back toward the rest area. "Sylvie and Achrotzyber can guard the Barracuda."

"Aren't you jealous at all?"

"A little, but that doesn't matter. Our partnership isn't founded on physical attraction. That would never work."

"And the sex with him doesn't mean anything to you?"

"It's wonderful when it happens, but I've got a few decades head start on him. My Companion has to collect experience with different partners so that he can please me better. I don't begrudge Sylvie at all."

Francine hesitated for a moment. "I guess it's more."

"He saved her life in an exceptional situation, I know. And that's after they already got physically acquainted with each other. I can see in her that she loves him."

"And you?"

"I won't force myself between them. I don't want to give Sylvie a reason to doubt their relationship, or for jealousy. We need Sylvie, and she needs Achrotzyber more than I do right now."

"But what will become of you?"

"Wait until tonight in Brisbane and I'll show you what becomes of me. That is, if you're willing to go manhunting with me."

"Do I look like a nun?"

CHAPTER FIFTEEN

The Sheikh was waiting for me in a small conference room in his hotel. When his secretary opened the door for me, the Sheikh walked toward me. He was dressed in his country's usual attire — the ankle-long white shirt and the headscarf with the bands, with the addition of a red-and-green-decorated black *bisht*.

"Legata Aurea Meier, welcome, welcome! Thank you very much for finding time for me so soon."

I offered him a hand, and he firmly took it. "I must thank you, Sheikh Rashid bin Khalifa — "

"Rashid, please. I'm not your ruler."

"Rashid, fine. My friends call me Jo."

He paused. Then he understood the hidden offer for friendship. "Jo, gladly. How was your travel here?"

"Perfect. I was a bit surprised to be picked up right on the airfield by a Rolls Royce, but there were no delays." From the moment we left the airport, a police escort led us to the hotel. At the reception, I learned of a suite booked for me. The suite doubtlessly offered room for two. I pointed to my side. "Francine, my pilot."

Francine made a curtsy when the Sheikh shook her hand, too. He briefly noted her brooch and pointed at two chairs and a small table behind him. Tea was ready at the table. "Knight Francine, I'm honored. Pardon me for being so thoughtless. I only prepared tea for two. Of course, the Legata Aurea's companion-in-arms is welcome."

"No problem, Rashid," she easily returned and fetched a

chair from the conference table. "I don't drink tea, and I can keep my mouth shut."

To spare the Sheikh the search for a polite phrase, I pointed at the chairs. We all gathered around the small table he had prepared. "Okay. Now, tell me what's on your mind."

Rashid placed his teacup down and leaned forward. "I have two big topics. Let's start with the short-term, yet still important, topic. You know that the United Nations have put me in charge of developing Earth's future defense forces for about a week now."

"Yes."

"That's currently a position without substance, but that shall change over the next week. I want to talk about it with you — with my supreme commander."

"Go ahead. I assume you already have a list of items?"

Rashid smiled. "Of course. But first I want to hear your assessment. Are we already done or not?"

"No, we're not. In my eyes, this attack wasn't the expected second wave."

"Why not?"

"There's some evidence. The recent entry point to our solar system was unusually close to our central star. Our researchers still have to recalculate that. Meanwhile, I hypothesize that it must be very difficult to target a wormhole across many light years. Following the laws of gravitational mechanics, there's always a risk that any such wormhole will arrive at the center of our solar system, unless you keep a huge safety margin."

The Sheikh spread his arms and glanced at Francine. "Gravitational mechanics is a foreign term for me. I'll simply have to believe you."

Francine just nodded.

"We only touched on that subject in our lessons, but the gravitational physics for envelope fields and wormholes follow the same principles," I explained.

"Well, well. The fact that you consider it unusual does it for me."

"Okay. Just as unusual was the way the wormhole was created. We could already prove that through comparisons with other wormholes."

"Wait, you can watch the Jellies' strategic movements?"

"Yes, sure. Oh, I think Martha hasn't found the time yet to finish the research report, but of course, those findings will be published."

"We shouldn't forget to discuss the strategic conclusions from these findings."

I nodded. "Martha is collecting all data for later analysis and assessment. That didn't have priority for us yet."

"Of course not. Is there any further evidence?"

"Yes. The crashed Scout's crew didn't consist of Jellies."

"I understand. What conclusion do you draw from that?"

"We still have to expect the second wave."

Rashid nodded and again glanced at Francine, then reached for his teacup. "And?"

Francine recognized what he was up to first. "There's at least one more spacefaring race on the raid. This brown pest was able to take a spaceship away from the Jellies and steer it through a wormhole to another inhabited system. So not only do we have to expect a second wave of Jellies but perhaps even another brown pest attack."

The Sheikh smirked. "Indeed. I presume you're taking the next step there. I hadn't considered another such attack yet."

Francine was visibly happy about the praise.

Rashid turned back to me. "We must make these findings the foundation for further planning, mustn't we?"

"Exactly."

"Then we can walk through my questions now."

CHAPTER SIXTEEN

"Let me use the classical setup," Rashid began again and placed his teacup down. "We need to cover the classical military branches, namely the army, navy, and air force. The army will mainly operate the armor suits. According to my information, there are currently two production locations. One is on your island, and the other is in the United States."

"That's correct."

"Is that advisable under strategic considerations?"

I was about to mention that strategy wasn't my favorite subject, but then again I was *supreme commander*. No — perhaps I wasn't good at it, but it surely was my subject. Besides, I wasn't entirely blank. My Analogy provided Zoe's *recollections* of the *Simulation*, a series of strategy workshops, which Zoe and her Companion used to train new officers. Moreover, many years ago they both had faced the same question.

"No," I replied accordingly. "I've made this decision purely opportunistically. I can't take the production away from the Americans while on my island, I needed and still need the means to produce new suits. At the time of mobilization, relocation was no longer advisable."

"Would more production lines distributed around the world be a better solution?"

"No, on no account."

"Why not? Is it advisable to risk that all sites fall into the enemy's hands?"

"That's not the point, but I understand where your question is leading. When it's about countering a Jelly invasion —

and now also a brown pest invasion — my strategy is based on an early defense. The enemy should not have the chance to establish a bridgehead and force us to withstand a campaign of attrition. I assume we can't afford rearguard action and guerilla tactics. Most importantly, we can't afford to sacrifice the majority of the population just to sustain the enemy's feeding habits. According to this strategy, we no longer have to worry about the production lines' locations from the moment of the enemy's touchdown."

Rashid nodded and placed the fingertips of both hands together. "That's conclusive. Do you think the current distribution of locations is optimal?"

"Yes and no. No, because I don't even know where the American production line is located. For the same reason, I say yes because I can say that both locations are secure. On my island, I can currently ensure a sufficient output of new suits for my needs, and the Americans have to procure the resources for their new suits themselves without burdening my budget. Honestly, Rashid — I alone, or my University, respectively, can't afford such a mobilization."

"No, of course not. It will be my task to ensure the funding for the production of our military equipment, as well as for recruitment. I will provide the necessary units for you. You can decide how to deploy them." He raised both hands.

"Of course, we will have counsel." Again, he glanced at Francine. "You already gathered a very competent team around you. So far, I've only hired a few quite efficient administrative helpers. After our conversation, I'll look for more consultants."

"Is there any other reason you're asking about locations?" I now dug deeper myself. "Or is it only the financial aspect?"

"No, not only. Of course, I will take care of the logistics, too, that is, making sure the new suits and their bearers meet. I will also have to make sure the men and women in those suits receive appropriate training. The locations' safety is dear to me, too. We both don't want to see such means of power abused for self-serving interests, do we?"

"Nicely put," I agreed. "Although that's exactly the reason for the current situation."

"Care to explain that comment?"

"Rashid, the reason the Americans now have a production line for armor suits isn't that I trust them, but because I needed their aid to reach my personal goals."

With this admittance, I had obviously caught him by surprise.

"Help with what goals?" he asked.

"Well, all this began with me winning an Ironman unplanned . . ."

CHAPTER SEVENTEEN

"Once the Cartel was decapitated with the Marines' assistance, I couldn't just take their suits and their newly gained production line away," I ended my story. "After that, I was busy with New York's liberation, which led to some jail time."

"Jail? Why?" Rashid asked.

"That's another long story. But do you understand now why the Americans have the suits?"

"Yes, I understand now. You have a very peculiar past."

"Eventually, you should have someone tell you the story about how she met us," Francine said. "That's far more peculiar."

"Yes. It's a strange career path for a Dragon empress."

I shrugged. "You should take into account that I met my Dragon Companion quite late and learned of my heritage much later." Rashid had a puzzled expression on his face, so I probably had to explain this part, too. "The knowledge was there all the time, but I didn't *remember* it. I simply didn't know what to look for in my memories. Have you ever recalled a song you've heard before after hearing a phrase that triggered your memory?"

"Yes."

"And without such a trigger?"

He slowly shook his head. "No. I think not."

"That's how our brain works. You need a cue to come up with associations from your memory."

"Nicely put." He frowned. "Well, the past can't be

46

changed. I'll have to accept the situation as it is."

I'd expected him to follow up on my brief explanation, but he didn't. "Rashid, what's your problem?"

He sighed. "Jo, politics may play a minor role from a Dragon's point of view, but it's among my tasks to win the approval and gain the active support of all countries, including the Islamic countries."

"Not least, your people."

"Naturally. My people will expect from me—from one of them—to create some balance, whatever that may be. If I cannot work with production, then I should at least be able to work with training and the deployment of new units."

"What do you need?"

"I need a clear sign that says, *Have a look, the Dragon empress is there for all of us, not just for the West.*"

"What would such a sign be? Give me an example."

"Well, we could—for example—deploy an infantry unit of armor suits in the Arabic world."

"I wouldn't have trouble with that," I said. "Do it, and I will declare that I expressly support this endeavor."

He slowly nodded.

"Rashid, I can tell that there's more on your mind. Speak openly to me."

"Yes, it's somewhat delicate. You know, our military regularly performs evaluations of the talents of our junior leaders. When you opened the University, we decided to fully support our students with their applications. We've been testing candidates for possible new Simulations as well since we weren't sure if you revived your predecessor's tradition."

"Perhaps I should. We need good officers."

"You definitely should."

Now I sighed. Another task on my bucket list! Setting up a war room simulation for training and evaluating officer candidates wasn't something I could delegate, at least not if it were to meet my predecessor's standard. Worse, it would require substantial time and effort.

"We challenged our candidates with the old tests. Only one candidate stood out among them all. Her test results were outstanding. Our military leaders believe she is the ideal choice for the deployment of a new United Nations infantry unit based in the Arabic world."

"But? The Order presented the preliminary criteria so anyone can apply."

"We didn't submit the application yet. Rejection would be embarrassing for the people involved. I wanted to talk with you first."

"Embarrassing? What's the problem?"

He briefly lowered his gaze, collected himself, then looked straight into my eyes. "It's my daughter Fatima. She just received her commission as officer. Her mother has passed away, so she's my only child. People might know that."

CHAPTER EIGHTEEN

So, his daughter, Fatima, was the top candidate. Yes, I understood how that could be a tricky situation. Too quickly, the accusation could arise that he was favoring his family.

"Rashid, we can't afford to ignore your best candidate for personal considerations. If we want to conjure up an armor suit unit out of nothing in the Arabic world, it needs a competent leader. And just as in the past, we need young, unspoiled officers who can learn something entirely new. She should submit her application."

My answer didn't seem to satisfy him. "Rashid, send her to me. I'll talk to her. If we get along, I'll make her the commandant of a unit directly reporting to me. Okay?"

"She's here in the hotel."

"Then we'll do it now."

"Right after our meeting?"

"No, call her, now. I want to clarify this topic now."

I glanced at Francine. "Try to find something to drink for us."

"Alcohol-free?" she asked with a side glance at Rashid.

"Whatever you find."

I turned back to my conversation partner. "Rashid, we don't get intoxicated with alcohol. It's one of the advantages of Dragon technology."

"Oh, please don't worry about me. I'm well aware of the fact that you don't follow my religion. Although I do appreciate your knowledge of it."

49

There was a knock on the door, and a young woman in a plain blue uniform entered. She immediately stood attention in front of me and saluted. "Lieutenant Fatima saba Rashid reports as ordered, Legata Aurea."

I waved back and pointed at the conference table. "Please take a seat, Fatima. I want to talk to you."

She sat down at the table with a straight back. Her brown eyes were sparkling with curiosity.

"Fatima, I'm Jo. As Dragon empress, I'm Earth's supreme military leader now. I've never attended a formal military academy, so I have never been trained in military protocols. I don't know what to make of the respective practices. You have to excuse my casual manners, especially if we are to work together in the future."

The corner of her mouth twitched, but she nodded briefly.

"Fatima, I've got a position to assign as battalion commandant of the armor suits, and you're a potential candidate."

"A battalion?" The words escaped her with awe. From the corner of my eye, I saw Rashid's surprised reaction, too.

"Yes. For the first line of defense against a possible invasion, Earth needs at least one battalion in America, one in the Asia-Pacific area, and one in the Europe-African-Arabic area. Of course, we'll start with just a platoon for now and a company later, but at the end—which we'll hopefully reach within the next five to ten years—the first platoon commandant will also be the first battalion commandant."

"That is—uh—surprising."

"I understand that you're unsure what to make of my offer. You only just received your commission, and we're already talking about the next three or four career steps. However, you'll have to get used to that if you want to collaborate with me. If we reach an agreement."

Instantly, she was alert again.

"Relax, Fatima, this is not a test. I'm being open with you, and I ask for open, honest answers in return. What do you know about the armor suits?"

"The armor suits cover the entire body with a layer of semi-organic, self-repairing material made of nanos. It protects the user from thrust weapons, firearms, and — in a limited way — from plasma rounds, too. The suit is equipped with amplifiers which provide the user with more bounce and agility. The amplifiers are powered by a micro fusion reactor in a back-pack. The backpack also contains the ammunition magazines for two linear cannons mounted under the arms. The suit's visor provides tactical information and three-sixty-degree vision. The radio automatically establishes a hierarchically structured connection between the units in which the data transmission is based on hard-to-locate, encrypted short impulses. The suits' most important feature, though, is it grants wearers the ability to blend into their surroundings."

"Nicely recited, Fatima, but I'm not sure if you fully grasp the idea of the suit."

Camouflage.

She gasped when I suddenly disappeared. Rashid said something in Arabic under his breath. Meanwhile, Francine — now lolling in her chair — only grinned.

With another thought, I became visible again. "The effect's truly good, but that wasn't what I'm after. Fatima, what do you know about armor suit units?"

"The smallest unit is a tandem team. Six tandem teams form a group. Three groups make a platoon, so that makes thirty-six soldiers. Three platoons make a company, three companies a battalion. There are no additional positions for officers, but those act within a tandem team position, too."

"Good, but we haven't arrived at the core yet. I'll give you a hint. Francine, can you just get up, please?"

"Sure." Francine stood up before her chair. "Like this?"

"Turn around once, slowly."

We watched her.

"Fatima, Francine wears quite a similar suit. As space pilot, she doesn't need camouflage or protection against firearms, but instead the suit protects against radiation and decompression. For everyday use, we dyed the nano-typical gold to black. The suit has no amplifiers and needs no backpack, but in principle, it's the same suit. What do you notice about the suit?"

"The suit fits perfectly."

"Exactly. Moreover, Francine doesn't wear anything under it, because that would only bug her. As a consequence, you can not only see that she's in good condition and her breasts need no support, but you can also see the shape of her vulva in every detail."

During this description, I watched Fatima. She blushed a little.

"Fatima, if you want to wear such a suit, you will be as visible."

"I-I think I can handle that."

"But that's not all. You must also be aware of the fact that each tandem team consists of one man and one woman?"

"Yes, of course."

Yes, of course, she knew that, but did she understand what that meant emotionally?

"The men wear the same skintight suits, too. You will be able to see every detail of the male anatomy. You learn to be comfortable with the male physique, because you'll have to help your tandem partner put the suit on and take it off. He will help you put your suit on and take it off as well. Also, when you're going to battle, you'll be traveling light—that is, tents are a luxury. If necessary, you'll have to take your suit off in front of your entire unit."

With every sentence, I reached deeper into her, and her eyes widened.

"Francine, thank you for now."

As Francine took her seat, I looked Rashid's only daughter straight in the eyes.

"Fatima, nudity should mean nothing to a member of the armor suit infantry. As leader of such a unit, you not only have to be an example, but you also must help your soldiers discard their inhibitions and focus on their job exclusively. Can you do that?"

This was a critical moment. Did she understand my question to the ultimate consequence?

She didn't say a word. Instead, she rose, stood next to the conference table and began to take her clothes off briskly.

Her father was about to protest, but when Francine placed one hand on his arm, he quietly leaned back into his chair again.

Fatima took off everything. She placed her clothes on the chair she had occupied before. Once she had put her knickers over the backrest, she stood at attention and saluted once again.

I glanced at her small breasts, the knot that was her belly-button and her flurry pubes. She didn't tremble. The only signs of her embarrassment were her half-closed eyelids and her gaze repeatedly twitching toward her father.

"Sit down."

I hadn't said a word about dressing, so she didn't do it.

"Fatima, let's talk about strategy. We assume a Jelly lander will touch down at the south end of the Suez Canal. It's your job to organize the defense. You command a company of armor suits and the Egyptian and Israeli military units. I can give you all details on strength and position, but that will cost you time. How do you proceed?"

CHAPTER NINETEEN

The Sheikh quietly watched the door close behind his completely dressed daughter. I had briefly considered sending her naked across the lobby to her room, but discarded the idea. For her first time, the poor girl had shown enough bravery.

"I very much hope she accepts," I said. I suspected that Fatima had made her decision already, though. For this role, she'd probably do anything. "She's got all she needs for this job."

"I didn't understand it," her father admitted.

"I did." Francine fetched a beer from the esky she had organized before the interview and tossed me another bottle. "Such exercises were part of our training. As an agent, you must be able to act even in the most embarrassing situations. Nudity is a weapon you can deploy against an enemy. It must not become a weapon the enemy can use against you. Okay, here it wasn't about how to use it as a weapon. It was about Fatima being able to focus on her job completely, personally communicate with high-rank officers, and quickly make the right strategic decisions without being distracted by her nudity, right?"

"Right," I confirmed. "I sincerely hope she never experiences such a situation in real life, but I want to be certain that a commandant in a dire position knows to tend to her people and the war first. Only later does she think of herself. This is what I expect from myself, too."

The Sheikh pulled at his collar. "It was a bit embarrassing

for me. She's my daughter, and I've never seen what a beautiful woman she's become. That's simply not appropriate."

"I know, Rashid. With your cultural background, it must be difficult to follow my way of thinking. The West has mostly shaken off the taboo of nudity, while your culture continues to enforce its strict rules on public modesty. I don't know what's better for society, but I do know that with the armor suits, pragmatism must come first."

"Yes, that's indeed an aspect I've spent too little considerations on so far. We will have to do a lot of persuasion."

It was important that he came to that conclusion. That was why I had let him attend this examination, after all. "It shouldn't be difficult for you to find a remote location for the training camp, would it? That way only armor suit wearers are affected first."

Then, an idea came to my mind. "Rashid, normally only military qualifications are considered when making teams. However, I think the new unit should have a tandem team that takes care of your people's mental health as well."

He was surprised by my comment. "You'd admit that?"

"That's only a proposal of mine. The unit's commander should decide the necessity of such a group herself. In my opinion, it's important that she has her unit combat-ready as soon as possible. If a company imam can help her with that, then I'm fine with it."

CHAPTER TWENTY

Francine handed Rashid a bottle of mineral water from the esky, and he thanked her with an impish smile.

"Water. That fits. The navy is my next topic. I think you haven't planned for specific units yet? Or am I mistaken?"

"Yes and no. No, my predecessor didn't leave me any plans for navy units. And no, I haven't thought about that topic myself either. But yes, we have built Frostdragon speedboats which can dive and fly. The boats are also suitable for military purposes. Some are even used on active duty by the American Coast Guard."

"That's a pity. We have high demands."

"Really? I didn't think so. Not until now."

Rashid drank some water and waited.

Francine spoke up. "It's about the Jelly Scouts, right? When they land in the water, we must be able to fight them. So we need units that can operate underwater. We'll also need an alternative to burning that will work underwater for the brown pest."

Rashid winked at her. "Thank you, Francine. That's exactly the problem. Well?"

I dug into my *recollections.* Could it be that Admiral-always-right April had entirely disregarded this problem? I didn't want to do my predecessor or her companion any injustice, as the invaders had come much too early for them to prepare. Surely, they had planned to upgrade the navy at some point. What else could I find? The name of a project—*Renaissance*—and accompanying plans. Most of it had remained a secret until their departure.

"Submarines. Zoe Lionheart's sons, the founders of Frost-dragon, designed carrier submarines. The respective data should still be in Frostdragon's databases like the information for the speedboats."

"Shouldn't that be known already?"

I had to dig for the answer to this question, too. "No. To the public, Frostdragon sold cars, plasma rifles, power generators, and those speedboats. That seems to have been a cover for the Lionheart sons' other activities. If nobody at Frostdragon uses the right search terms, the designs for the submarines won't come up. A few of the former company leaders might still know about it. When the Cartel took over, it's possible that these people quietly descended into hiding. Quite appropriate."

"Would *these people* answer a public announcement?"

"We'd have to test that theory. But as I know what to look for, I can just take care of it. This way, when I make the announcement, I only have to create an implementation team."

"Which you can leave to me, then. I am curious about these carrier submarines, though. They sound bulky and slow. What would these submarines carry?"

"Taipans. In principle, these fighters can be deployed underwater, too—oops, that bit only just came up as well. Okay, the boundary between navy and air force blurs. Moreover, the Phoenix carriers will become faster once we equip them with a nestle field drive."

"How big are they?" Francine asked.

"Large enough for an entire Taipan squadron."

"Cool. If we equip these things with a nestle field, we can make them ready for space like the *Mark Two*. Can't we? Then we could use the Taipans to chase Scouts behind the moon without Zoé having to wet her pants." She caught Rashid's indignant gaze and giggled. "Sorry."

The Sheikh didn't bother to comment. Instead, he continued his conversation with me, as if Francine hadn't spoken at all.

"I assume these carrier submarines are expensive and need some time for construction. I will assemble a team for this project, and we'll start once you can provide the plans. What about underwater weapon systems?"

"As far as I know, there are no Lionheart plans. We have to start from scratch."

"Is that primarily a Dragon technology problem?"

"That's primarily a question of coming up with the right ideas. Whether Dragon technology can help will emerge later."

"Then I'll summon an interdisciplinary team to gather ideas."

It was a relief that the Sheikh took most topics over himself. Only, how could he do that?

"What about the funding?"

"Don't worry. I have a budget to pay the people and a strategy for how to fund the actual construction. If the United Nations doesn't extend our budget, I'll propose to find private investors for our endeavors. I'm sure the big powers won't like that. They'll come around."

"We must secure the factories. That won't be easy," Francine chimed in again. "Not that this other party develops bad ideas."

Rashid pricked his ears. "What other party?"

"Didn't you hear anything about the assassinations?" I asked.

"Yes, of course. Something about a Japanese Dragon cult was mentioned."

"Those, too, but I'm not worried about them currently. We still don't know who sent the last team — and some of the ones before them. There's something bigger going on, with multiple factions playing their game."

The Sheikh leaned back. "Tell me all."

CHAPTER TWENTY-ONE

I found it astonishing that Rashid didn't take notes while I recapped the events of the past two years. Or did he have a recorder somewhere? When I finished, he clasped his hands and said, "I understand why setting the production lines up in an easy-to-shield location is favorable, now. It will make the logistics harder, though. We will need to consult your people so we can all reach an acceptable standard."

"And armor suits to guard the facility," Francine proposed.

Rashid nodded at her. "We have to use the infantry for guard service, too. That's good, since we'll have at least one meaningful task for these people besides training. The hardest problem will be to ensure the factory staff's integrity. We can't have spies there."

"Yes." I pondered whether I could spot possible agents with my skills in gambling.

"That won't be your problem," the Sheikh interrupted my thoughts. "Soldier training, production, the safety of production sites, and funding are my job. I wasn't assigned to this post to unload my problems on you, but the reverse. The Australians made that very clear, and I support this approach. Let's talk about the air force now. We're already quite advanced in this field. There's a construction program for an aircraft, and we only have to expand the foundations. There's a preliminary pilot selection program set-up—where, by the way, your friends have done a great job, if I may say so. From my point of view, it can be sustained for the next thirty to forty years before someone manages to find faults with it."

"Thank you," I said. "I will pass that on. But we don't have a place for the air school and no curriculum yet. Jenny and Zoé will surely be able to patch something together, but—"

Rashid raised a hand. "As I said, that's my problem. You find the teachers. I'll find them the assistants and consultants they need. I'll tell my air force attaché to turn to Jenny and Zoé. Will their first name suffice to find them?"

"If he asks for Knight Jenny and Knight Zoé, nothing can go wrong," Francine added.

"Good. I have one other question about the air force. Your Taipans still need a weapon system that can be used against a Jelly lander, right?"

I had to focus my thoughts to maintain my poker face. "We have a concept for this purpose that's not sufficiently mature, but eventually it can be fitted into a Taipan weapons bay. It's going by the working title of *cake knife* since that name resembles its function. The lander would be the cake in this case."

Rashid raised his eyebrows. "That would be quite a weapon indeed. You said it's just a concept?"

"The only working prototype is installed on our Barracuda. With it, we fought the mothership." I focused my gaze on him. "I'm very worried about this weapon getting into the wrong hands."

Could I trust Rashid with information on the cake knife and our disruptor torpedo?

My gaze rested on his open, friendly face. I'd put the question the wrong way. What could he do with this knowledge? What damage could he do, and which mistakes could he make out of ignorance if I didn't let him in?

He seemed honest to me, and if I couldn't trust him, I'd have to insist on his instant replacement.

So it was decided. He had to know it.

CHAPTER TWENTY-TWO

Rashid clasped his hands, startling me out of my reverie, and nodded contentedly. "Good. So we don't need a marine infantry, but only additional training for zero-G and some extra gear for the armor suits. That way we can save on instructors."

"And on additional stress when we begin setting up the new unit, too." Francine juggled an empty beer bottle. "Questions of who'll be the leader of a new unit, where it should be located, and so on. I wouldn't want any of those political problems. Solving all of that in one lifetime is impossible."

"The word *impossible* is not in the leaders' dictionaries. No matter how big the challenges, strong faith, determination and resolve will overcome them," Rashid said. "At least that's what my great-grandfather said."

"Who was your great-grandfather?" Francine asked.

"His Highness Sheikh Mohammed bin Rashid Al Maktoum."

"His Highness?" I asked. Moreover, the name rang a bell. I must've heard it back then during my visit to Dubai.

"He was our head of state." Rashid smiled. "We owe many achievements to him."

"Then you're a member of the ruling family," I concluded.

"The third in succession to the throne," Rashid admitted. "But, please, that shouldn't matter to us. After all, you're a ruler yourself."

"Of a tiny island."

"And of the only Dragon Technology University on this

planet. Don't forget that."

No, I couldn't forget that. Nor could I forget that only two hours earlier I encouraged a princess to undress completely.

Now that I was no longer questioning her, I could contemplate how sweet her large brown eyes had appeared, her firm small breasts, and most of all her dense little fur.

"What are you thinking of?" Rashid asked.

"Of your daughter."

"Oh, don't worry about that. Just the opposite. My daughter is fighting with all her power against the constraints of such a position. That's why she joined the military. She hoped to gain a position there on her own, and I may proudly claim that she managed to do it."

"Now even more," Francine agreed.

"Speaking of her achievements . . ." I focused on Rashid. "You may quote me on this. If anyone even insinuates that she owes her new position to personal relationships, I'll personally tear that person's head off. Her only advantage was to get an earlier interview date."

The Sheikh smiled. "I'd prefer a less drastic phrasing. You might come into the tight spot of having to implement such a threat."

I smiled back. "I keep my promises."

His smile froze.

"Okay, Rashid." I made a stern face. "Then propose to anyone who dares to accuse me of playing favorites with your daughter to come and tell me their accusations right to my face. Otherwise, they should remain silent about the topic. At least, until they've gathered enough courage to face me."

"They won't do it."

"Tell their accusations to my face?"

"They won't approach you, but they won't remain silent either."

"Then I will come to them, to the United Nations. I'll

personally ask them to talk to me about the allegations they believe I committed or I'll call them cowards."

"That won't work."

"Why not?"

"You have no right to speak at the United Nations."

"Oh." I pondered that for a moment. "Formally, you're right. In that case, I'm sorry. There's no basis for collaboration between the two of us."

Rashid raised an eyebrow. "Until a couple of minutes ago, I thought we got along well with each other."

"It's nothing personal. But I can only collaborate with the United Nations Secretary for Interstellar Defence as the Administrative Commander of the United Nations Defence Forces if my relationship with the United Nations is clarified. I'm the head of the exclave Velvet Island, and I claim a seat and the right to vote in the United Nations."

Now Rashid smiled again. "Oh yes, but of course!"

"Moreover, as Dragon empress, I claim the respective seat and vote in the Security Council. There's a precedent for that."

Rashid obviously knew about my predecessor's claim for such a seat, otherwise he'd have asked. "The Lionheart terminated all Dragon contracts with the UN before they departed."

"No. Humans unilaterally canceled all contracts with the Dragons after the Invasion's first wave. No, canceled is the wrong word. Humans violated the contracts. If I continue to do this job, I expect all contracts to be back in effect without further negotiations."

Rashid swallowed hard. "How will we cross-check that?"

I tapped my head. "I don't merely have technical knowledge in my head, but also the wording of every single agreement. Tell the UN that I will notice any tricks. If I find any, I will consider it as a betrayal."

"That sounds like a threat."

"We're at war, Rashid. Think about it." I nodded at Francine. "It's been a long day. Would it be okay if we continue tomorrow morning?"

PART FOUR—MERRIMENT

CHAPTER TWENTY-THREE

Francine pressed the elevator button and looked down at me. "You tossed him quite a chunk to nibble there."

"Yes, I did," I admitted. "Perhaps I should've started our conference with it, but the idea just came up."

"Your standards are quite high."

"A seat and the right to vote won't grant me a majority, but the right to veto, at least. With that, I can prevent irrelevant decisions from being passed."

From the corner of my eye, I saw a familiar shape approaching, but I continued my conversation with Francine.

"Maybe it's because I'm an anarchist. I can't stand someone telling me what to do. Enough of that. Let's put work aside for tonight and figure out how we can have a fun evening."

I turned to face the familiar figure hovering behind me. "Oh, hello, Fatima!"

The young officer saluted. "Imperatrix Aurea."

"Stop with the formal stuff. I already told you I'm not a military person. I'm Jo, and that's Francine. What can I do for you?"

"Jo, I don't think I should miss the opportunity to get to know my future superior better. Who knows when the events will leave us time for that again?"

Francine made a doubtful face.

I winked at her and focused firmly on Fatima's eyes. "Fatima, your future superior and her pilot are going out tonight. We are determined to consume significant amounts of alcohol and have wild, uninhibited intercourse with total strangers.

Depending on the circumstances, we might even have a three-some or foursome."

She didn't lower her gaze in embarrassment or blush. Instead, I noticed she was breathing a little more heavily, and her pulse was steadily accelerating. Her pupils were dilated, too.

I couldn't see whether her nipples hardened as well — probably because of her uniform. She couldn't hide the tremble in her voice, though.

"I will not let this opportunity pass. My commandant is a product of the Western world. I must learn to know her lifestyle to understand her motivations. To that end, I will do whatever is necessary."

"What does your religion say or what does your father say about this?"

"My religion says women shall be obedient to their husbands. I, however, will command. A long time ago — before I joined the military — I told my father that the day would come when I will dispose of my body without his approval. This is my business alone."

"There could be side effects," Francine said as she entered the elevator. Fatima and I followed her inside. Francine pressed the button for our floor and briefly glanced at Fatima, who didn't make a single comment on her destination or the side effects.

"I guess we can take precautions. Fatima, the alcohol doesn't matter here. It doesn't have an intoxicating effect on Francine and me. We only drink for the taste. You don't have to drink tonight. It won't tell you anything about us."

"Oh, good."

We reached our floor and headed to our suite. Fatima followed us.

"Where's your room?" I asked.

"One floor below."

"You should take a shower and put on something else."

"Oh. I didn't bring anything else."

"Me neither," Francine said.

I rolled my eyes. "Where can you find any gear this late in Brisbane?"

"I'll ask the concierge," Francine proposed. "Perhaps he knows someone who'd open up his shop again for the Imperatrix Aurea. Meanwhile, I propose that you, Fatima, take a shower with us. It will be helpful if we explain a few more things to you before we leave."

CHAPTER TWENTY-FOUR

Fatima was still innocent when Francine pushed her into the bathroom. She didn't expect anything but a shower. After all, Francine and I had seen her naked before.

All three of us were nude, but Fatima still didn't suspect anything. After all, it was natural to undress for a shower, and there wasn't much of a difference between our naked bodies and our skintight suits.

The shower in our suite was spacious enough for the three of us, so Fatima didn't think anything of it when we all entered together.

I began to soap Francine, and she began to treat our new hire. Naturally, she didn't leave out Fatima's breasts. Soon, her victim's nipples became hard again.

"Let's talk about where being touched feels good," I whispered as I caressed her bum cleft's upper end.

Fatima was breathing heavily by now.

"You should know your body before meeting a man, and you should know what you want. He should at least dedicate enough of his time to make you ready."

My greatest advantage was that I didn't have to bend down to suck her dark nipples, which made Fatima moan.

"That's a very sensitive spot," Francine commented. "You should be grateful that men like to play with them so much."

My victim didn't know where to place her arms, so I directed them to my breasts.

"Try to sense how good that can feel so that you understand why men strive for them."

Fatima was wet, and not just from the water, I could tell by the smell of her juice. I winked at Francine. She reached around our guest from behind and caressed the side of the breast's base.

"If you feel you're ready, allow him to expand his treatment." Francine reached further around while she continued to explain and I sucked Fatima's nipples.

"Guide his tender hands to your hips and let him explore your waist. Give him the opportunity to hold your firm bum."

I assumed this part, whereby I pulled her buttocks far apart.

Francine's hands wandered forward under my arms. "The insides of your upper legs are particularly tender and sensitive. He'll soon explore your mons and your fluffy pubes. Your outer labia's closed, so open your legs wide."

Fatima obediently placed her feet outward, opening herself up to Francine's exploring fingers.

"Yes, exactly. Do you feel them separate? Do you feel the cool air reaching your intimate parts? A little more — yes — and your inner labia opens, too."

Perhaps Francine helped a little by pulling the skin apart on both sides. In any case, Fatima was heavily panting by now. Her hands groped my boobs hard.

"You're particularly sensitive there. The most responsive parts are a bit deeper inside your vagina and above, where your labia meets your clitoris."

Francine was now probing to see if she was wrong. She wanted to see if the young woman might be mutilated but seemed to find no evidence for it. Instead, the touch sufficed to make Fatima come.

"A man will rarely achieve that," I explained to her after she had regained her breath. "Instead, he'll penetrate your slippery vagina with his erect penis and stimulate the responsive parts inside."

"It will hurt the first time," Francine said. "Are you still untouched?"

"Not anymore," Fatima wheezed.

"By a man?"

"Oh. Well, no. I never had a man." Fatima held Francine's hand. "Give me a chance to experience a man on my own. There's thrill in surprise, too. Right?"

"Sure." I spotted a dab of soap foam and blew it away. "Well, we should towel off before . . ."

There was a knocking at our suite's door. I shrugged and left the task of shedding water to my nanos. Another mental command helped me into my black suit. Then I was ready to open the door.

A man in a loud red jacket looked up past my head. He lowered his gaze when he registered that I wasn't taller than him. Behind him were two young ladies pulling a clothes rack on wheels that held numerous items of clothing. There was a third woman with a large plastic container on wheels next to the rack.

"Madame Meier?"

"Yes."

"Good evening. Ernesto Moretti, at your service. You requested new evening attire?"

"For my two companions and myself, yes. Come in."

I cleared the way and let the small caravan pass.

Ernesto stayed with me. "We only brought a small sample to clarify the direction of your desires."

"Well, we want to dress up for a night in the city," I began.

Francine appeared in the open doorway to the bathroom, stark naked. "It can be somewhat daring. It shouldn't appear cheap, though."

Ernesto's heartbeat immediately accelerated, but his voice remained firm. "Naturally." He waved at one of his assistants, and she fetched an asymmetric crimson red cocktail dress from the rack. "This should fit you excellently."

"I'm not sure," Francine began. "I should perhaps wear something with pants."

I knew that she was considering her ease of movement, not the fashion point of view.

"Out of the question." Ernesto shook his head. "Not for an evening event. That would be a severe faux pas. A more conservative combination would be possible, but pretty uncommon already."

"Try it on," I encouraged her.

Francine stepped forward, stepped into the dress and pulled the single strap over her right shoulder. The assistant pulled up the zipper on the opposite side. The left shoulder remained free, and in exchange, the left knee was covered and the right one free.

The third woman placed a pair of matching crimson red stilettos for Francine to wear.

"Perfect!" Ernesto praised. I could only agree with him. The dress hugged Francine's toned body marvelously. The color blended well with her brunette hair, and the overall impression was indeed breathtaking. "We have a matching lace ensemble . . ."

"I don't need it," Francine disrupted him. "As you said, it's perfect. Jo?"

"Perfect."

"As you wish." Ernesto was too professional to admit his liking, but aside from the erotic aspect, in my opinion, such dresses simply had to be worn pure. Under a skin-tight dress, there shouldn't be any panty lines. This one didn't leave many options except for a C string or a pasted piece of fabric.

"It was surely not just luck that the dress was the right size?" I asked. "The shoes, too."

Ernesto smiled. "The concierge has an excellent eye for proportions and could give me a good description."

"You appeal to him," I commented toward Francine.

She only smiled. "Your turn."

"Black or green?" the Maestro asked.

I had already spotted the tail of a green, semi-transparent fabric. "Green."

The assistant took it and held the short dress out to me, the fabric of which shimmered in the room light and changed between light and dark green.

"It might be a bit too daring," Ernesto said.

"Tut." My black dress slid to the floor upon my command. I allowed one of Ernesto's assistants to help me into the green dress. She closed the clasp of the high collar that held the upper part first. Then she secured the puffy shoulder parts to my upper arms with little bows. The back remained completely free, and the front part flowed over my chest in numerous pleats. Around the waist, it hugged me tightly, only to drop from my hips toward the knees in soft plaits at many different lengths without actually reaching them.

"We could perhaps look for matching underwear," Ernesto proposed.

"Nonsense." I stepped before a large mirror and examined the result. Yes, okay, my breasts were vaguely recognizable, depending on the lighting, as was my dark pubic hair, but at the same time, it looked quite natural to me.

"Like a fairy," Francine said. "You should remain barefoot for the best effect."

"We have something appropriate," the Maestro said and waved again. His shoe assistant reached deep into the box and produced sandals with gauzy green straps and extremely high golden stiletto heels. "Not quite like barefoot, but they make you taller. That eases the choice of dancing partners."

The sandals looked great, and they looked even better under my feet, even though I was almost standing on the tips of my toes. The balance was no big deal for me. I floated a few times around our suite and enjoyed the appropriate amount of admiration.

CHAPTER TWENTY-FIVE

"You had mentioned two companions?"

Ernesto was right. Poor Fatima was trapped in the bathroom. Our fashion show was keeping her separated from her underwear. It would've been inappropriate to demand that she appear nude in front of strangers for no reason.

Ernesto's gaze turned to the bathroom door, and an enchanted smile crossed his face.

Fatima was standing there, stark naked, with an expression of juvenile innocence Francine and I could never reproduce. She spotted the clothes rack and ambled up to it. "Oh, is there something for me, too?"

I didn't even want to know how she had managed to overcome her inhibitions so naturally or how long she had required to assume this state. She wasn't merely nude. She was simply there, as far away from stirring indecent ideas as possible. That made her even more erotic in my eyes.

One of Ernesto's assistants showed her a black cocktail dress, which was transparent except for a few strategic areas. She turned it down with a simple flick of her wrist. "Please! I don't want to go out in the nude!"

Instead, she pointed at a black dress at the end of the rack. "How about that one?"

The other assistant immediately pulled it out — a sleeveless, high-necked sheath dress of thin soft fabric that reached almost to the knee and had only one narrow but deep cleavage in the front.

Fatima nodded and allowed the assistant to help her with

it. It fit like a glove.

Ernesto's third helper was already holding two pairs of black shoes for her — both as high as the ones Francine and I wore. Fatima didn't notice the woman holding the shoes, though. She was busy marveling at herself in the mirror.

"It's perfect, isn't it?" she asked, and pulled at her cleavage.

"You're right," Francine confirmed. "As it is now, it's perfect. No bra, no string. Classical."

"The shoes are missing," I said. "Sandals, but not that high. Better low and safe to walk in than high and wobbly. You've got no experience there, or do you, Fatima?"

"N-n-no."

The assistant in charge of shoes offered Fatima a pair of high heels that were only five centimeters high. They had a narrow strap around the ankle and a little knob between the big and the next toe. Fatima tried them on and beamed.

"Comfy?" I asked.

"Yes. It's almost like I'm barefoot."

"You feel good, don't you?"

"Yes."

"That's the point." I winked at Ernesto. "I'm extraordinarily pleased. I think we can go and paint Brisbane now. How much is everything?"

"Oh, that's taken care of. You don't have to worry about it."

"Really? Thank you."

"No, I must thank *you*. It's an honor and a special privilege to be allowed to outfit the Imperatrix Aurea."

CHAPTER TWENTY-SIX

Francine took a deep breath once the door closed behind Ernesto and his assistants. "Cool. Everything's taken care of."

"My father took care of it," Fatima said. "The bill's on him. No matter what it is. That's common procedure."

"Great. I was starting to wonder if we could put it on a tab. Or do you have cash, Jo?"

"Me? No. In space, you don't need cash, and I haven't been back to the island since our return. But that's not a problem."

I held up a credit card in my hand—a perfect copy made from my nanos that would pass any security inspection. I didn't have any bad feelings about it, as I owned the card. The original just happened to be somewhere on the island. "So we're ready to go, ain't we?"

"What? No." Fatima disagreed very firmly. "I'm not coifed or made up, and neither are you. This can't be."

Francine drove her fingers through her short hair. "I always wear it like this."

"Tut-tut. Give the girls downstairs a chance to drain my father of some money, too. We haven't made a table reservation anywhere, right?"

"No." I would've ventured out randomly. Now that we were dressed up so tastefully, though, we should spoil ourselves at a likewise classy restaurant. I dialed the concierge with the room phone.

"Hello. I'm Johanna Meier."

"I know, Mrs. Meier. What can I do for you?"

"We need a dinner table for three. Something really good. We'd like to make a quick visit to the hairdresser before leaving, if that's possible."

"Of course. I already expected that. The Maestra is ready anytime it suits you."

"We'll be downstairs in a few minutes."

"Wonderful. May I order a taxi for later? The table at *Amanda* will be ready for you then."

"*Amanda?*"

"You will like it."

"I'm sure I will. I just wanted to know whether *Amanda* is the venue's name or the proprietor's."

"It's both."

"Thanks. By the way, Ernesto was perfect. We're about to come downstairs."

Francine gave me a questioning look when I disconnected.

"What?" I asked.

"He was well prepared, wasn't he? I bet he made the table booking when Rashid ordered the room for us."

"Rashid didn't know how soon we'd take up his invitation."

"No. But since we came here, it was clear."

"Nobody could be sure we'd stay overnight."

"Still, we have a suite."

"Nobody could guess we'd go out for dinner."

"Nobody knew when the Jellies would come, but there were still plans."

Francine pushed Fatima toward the door. "Let's go. Jo, our meal will only be prepared after we order. However, a good concierge will be prepared for any desire the Imperatrix Aurea could voice and have a table prepared for you at the city's best venue. Amanda and Basil . . ."

"Basil?"

"Yes, Basil. That's the name of the concierge. Amanda and Basil must have made an agreement with each other. That means two things."

"First?" I asked and followed the two to the elevator. The room door fell shut behind us.

"First, it means that anyone in this city who considers himself important has a reservation there tonight, too. Some may have even made reservations for several nights in a row. They all hope to hit the jackpot, which is to see you."

Fatima tried to say something, but I was faster than she was.

"Second?"

"It also means anyone targeting you knows exactly where to look for you."

My pilot let us enter the elevator first. "But of course the security staff knows that, too. After all, we're all here officially."

"I'd say, the three of us can handle anything that could come for us. Or, Fatima?"

The young woman gazed at me in surprise. "The three of us?"

"You haven't told me your decision yet. But for tonight, we're a team. Aren't we?"

"Yes, but . . ." She looked down.

"You're a trained soldier and have your officer commission. You have no reason for false modesty. Later in the taxi, I'll tell you a bit more about how Dragons collaborate."

"Yes. Okay."

"What else bothers you?"

"What Francine said—the people—I admit I had thought we'd go out in private." She looked at her naked toes and pulled at her cleavage.

Francine turned away with a grin.

I pointed at myself. "If one of us is dressed daringly, it's me. Your dress is extremely decent. One thing, though, a lady shouldn't pluck at her dress all the time."

"Oh. Of course."

"Imagine it's an armor suit. Or better yet, imagine that you're a role model. Wear your dress with pride."

Fatima briefly closed her eyes, took a deep breath and straightened herself. When she looked at me again, she had at least outwardly shed all her bashfulness. "Yes, *Protectress.*"

Francine twitched three times, but fought her silent laughter down and became stern again. The elevator had reached its destination. "Our entrance."

Chapter Twenty-seven

The hair stylist despaired when she saw Francine and me. When Fatima entered, a little hope shimmered through.

I shrugged. "We haven't had much time for ourselves since our return from space."

She raised both hands up to her mouth. "Oh! Sorry—uh—*Protectress.*" Then she bowed. "I'm truly sorry. For a moment I had forgotten the burden you have carried and continue to carry for us."

"Perhaps that's due to Ernesto's good work. I understand that we're a true challenge for your artistry, and I appreciate your efforts."

Now a smile was playing around the corners of her mouth. "My ladies and I are ready to accept the challenge."

"So," she announced about one hour later, after her hair designers, makeup artists, and manicurists had run riot on us. She turned my chair around to face the mirror. "Now I can let you go out in public."

Was that really me?

The woman in the mirror was such a beauty. I could reasonably claim that I traveled around the world—including the world of the rich and beautiful—but the woman sitting opposite me was the prettiest thing I'd ever seen. There was nothing even remotely comparable to her, even in Cannes or Las Vegas.

Okay, that sounds quite narcissistic. But my *Analogy* supported the judgment before it confirmed for me that this face in the mirror was indeed mine.

Here I was, an experienced whore and escort, a rich gambler, the urbane Dragon empress, who knew every trick in the book. For the first time, I saw what a true artist could make of this raw material.

Going to a salon was indeed a novelty in my life. I had never visited a hairdresser before. Coworkers usually cut my hair, or I cut it myself. I would try to give my hair some shape or simply let the short strands stick out. The same was true for makeup. I used it sparingly. It had always looked okay, and men liked it.

Francine and Fatima were still busy admiring themselves in the mirror when I looked up to our Maestra.

"It's unique," I said.

"Thank you. I'm glad you like it."

"It surely won't remain that way."

"Oh, of course not. But pictures of it will spread around the world tomorrow. The paparazzi will make sure of that."

"Paparazzi?"

"Photographers."

"Oh, thanks. I know the term, only . . ." Only I'd never been the target of this kind of attention before. Being photographed or filmed as Dragon empress was common now, but people after a picture of me as a human, as a woman was new. The paparazzi were unknown to me. People who were interested in taking photos up young ladies' skirts to see if these ladies wore panties, which they wouldn't find with us, were going to be a challenge.

I could stand by that. My dress didn't hide much. Francine would be amused and open her thighs a bit wider.

Fatima's father couldn't find his daughter's pubes printed in all the newspapers the next morning amusing. I had to do something about that.

"Do you have glitter?"

"That would be . . ."

"Not for my hair," I interrupted. "For a little surprise. Glitter and some powder."

CHAPTER TWENTY-EIGHT

The photographers got more than they bargained for when we arrived at *Amanda*. In the taxi, I told Francine about the paparazzi. She reacted the way I expected, by making sure her labia was glistening wet.

"That will distract them from you," she told Fatima.

I placed one hand on Fatima's arm. "Francine will go first, and I'll follow. Place your legs out of the car when I stretch my arm out to you. If you keep your knees together when I help you out, nobody will spot anything. I've prepared a little trick."

The little trick was a mixture of powder and glitter, refined by my nano manipulators. I blew the powder on my hand toward the photographers upon exit to create a curtain of reflecting metal particles for several seconds, which mirrored each flash a thousand-fold back to the cameras, making the pictures useless. By the time the curtain reached the ground, Fatima had already finished walking the red carpet Amanda had rolled out for us.

My precaution turned out to be unnecessary. The lenses remained focused on me, just as did the microphones. Many reporters yelled their questions at me. I ignored them all as we walked down the red carpet and climbed the steps to the entrance. When I reached the top of the stairs, I waved at Francine and pushed Fatima inside the restaurant. Then I turned around to face the cameras. When I spread my arms, everyone fell silent.

"Folks, this is my very first opportunity for a decent dinner since my return," I said out loud for all the microphones.

"The only thing I can tell you now is that I met an excellent wardrobe stylist and a talented hairdresser with their teams in Brisbane."

"When?" someone from the third row yelled. "More?"

"When I can tell you more? Perhaps the day after tomorrow. I'll go for a jog. Anyone who can keep up with my pace can ask me questions. But I'm warning you. I'll run a full forty-two kilometers."

Chapter Twenty-nine

A *manda's* staff was attentive and unobtrusive. The food and wines were exquisite. It took some effort to touch the marvelously decorated food, but after the first bite, it was hard not to scarf. In return, the waiters found it difficult not to sneak a peek at our female assets.

The other male guests felt the same. After dessert, several gentlemen came to our table to talk to us. They didn't look like suitors, though. They all had female company. Eventually, Francine prevented guests from approaching our table with one glance.

"You're good at that," I praised her.

"What?"

"Your razor-sharp glare. If you scrutinized your meal like that, you wouldn't need a knife."

Fatima laughed out loud.

Francine briefly frowned, then smiled, too. "I don't think they're coming here to ask for our hairdresser's name."

"No. They're lobbyists, and I don't want to entertain such conversations tonight."

An older lady in a white evening pantsuit wouldn't be deterred from reaching us. She looked as if she owned the venue. She had to be the boss.

"Good evening, Protectress," she said as she approached me. She turned to my dinner dates as well and said, "Ladies." She hardly gave us time to give her a friendly nod before she introduced herself. "I'm Amanda. Was everything to your liking?"

I glanced at my companions briefly, read approval on both their faces and smiled at Amanda. "Our expectations were met to our utmost satisfaction. You may quote that."

Her eyes flashed.

"I very much hope not too much time will pass before our duties allow us another visit. Now we only have two little wishes left."

"Sure. What can I do for you?"

"First, I'd like to have the bill, please. Second, I'd like a route out of here where the press can't follow us. I don't want to have to call my spaceship for that."

The restaurant owner smiled. "You're my guests. I can't, and I won't take money from people who put their lives at stake for us all. Once you're ready to leave, just tell me."

"We're ready."

"Okay, follow me."

We rose together and followed Amanda to the back, past the bathrooms, through a door labeled *Private,* up some stairs, and through a heavy steel door to another staircase.

"We're in the next house now. Come with me." Two floors below, she led us through another steel door into a garage. "Okay. Through that door over there you'll reach a house in the next street. Take the normal exit to the front, and you should remain unspotted. Even the clever reporters waiting at my back door shouldn't know this way."

"Thank you."

"As I said. I must thank you. Whatever you're up to, have fun."

CHAPTER THIRTY

W e probably could have stopped any car with our attire, but we preferred a taxi. Francine took the front seat, while Fatima and I snuck into the back.

"Where do you want to go?" the driver asked. "To the casino?"

"We're looking for a waterhole," Francine said.

"Waterhole?"

"We want to visit this city's most questionable nightclub. The place where there's truly something going on, where we can meet the tough guys."

"Oh. Well, okay." His gaze was fixated on Francine's right thigh. "You really want that? There are a few rough pubs in the Riverdowns."

"Sounds good. Get going."

He pulled away from the curb and stepped on the brakes to let another car pass, then merged the taxi with traffic. "That's no place for young ladies."

"We're not looking for a place for ladies, but entertainment for soldiers on leave, okay?"

"Oh. That's something else. Air Force?"

"Special Forces. Lone warriors."

"Oh, well."

"Tell us something about Riverdowns. I don't know that quarter yet."

"No? Ah, so you're not from this area, right? It's a part of the old harbor zone industry. Originally, it was just a few empty warehouses where the unemployed met. Then the youth gangs, hustlers, whores, and dealers came. Well, the police cleaned it up before the place became too bad, but it's still a quite rough place."

"Sounds exciting."

"Um. Won't you get into trouble with your superiors if you get into a brawl or something?"

Francine grinned. "Only if we lose."

"And that won't happen," I added from the back.

"How can you be so sure?" the driver asked. "The guys here are strong. A few of them know how to use a knife. Aw, forget it. This isn't my business."

"Still, thanks for caring," Francine said. "But it's no problem."

"Down there?" Francine asked when we turned onto an unlit side road, at the end of which a group of people had assembled before one of the warehouses.

Our driver proceeded cautiously.

"Yes."

"We'll get off here and walk the rest of the way."

"If you like." He stopped at once and took a deep breath. *Relieved?* "I can wait here for a moment."

"That won't be necessary," I said and handed him my credit card.

He gave it a quick glance and was about to swipe it into his reader, then he paused, read the name again and turned around. "*The* Johanna Meier?"

I smiled, cocked my head, and shrugged.

He returned the smile. "Okay, no. You surely won't have trouble here."

I trusted him not to give the press a hint. To bring up the subject seemed wrong to me.

His device accepted my fingerprint. Then he handed me the card back. "Have fun!"

"Thanks."

We exited and waited until he turned his taxi around and drove away.

"Looks interesting," I said to Francine. "Good choice. But we're not here to look for trouble, are we?"

"That would be up to you. No, we're not looking for trouble or a training partner for Fatima."

She gazed at our companion. "We'll get an impression here of how the current situation appears to the common people and whether we have to expect trouble here. Our favorite enemies must do their recruitment somewhere. Moreover, I'm up for a beer and a hard fuck, not champagne and candlelight romance. Uh, Fatima, you don't have to do the same. That's clear, yeah?"

"I came here for a specific purpose, Francine. I want to know my superior and her way of life. I've already seen how she wines and dines. Now it's time for a wild night. I know this won't often happen, okay, and that's why I'm joining you, come what may. I'm a soldier, and I won't chicken out, neither from a battle where a bullet could penetrate me, nor from a man whose cock could penetrate me."

Francine raised an eyebrow.

I could only admire the young woman for her bravery, even though her voice slightly trembled. It surely wasn't that easy to shed her education and her beliefs, but I wouldn't hold her back. Anyone who'd go into close combat with Jellies together with a tandem partner had to be able to give up everything else. That was the standard I expected, at least.

"Watch out for knives that could be a threat to us," I warned. "Fatima, I assume you can defend yourself. Right?"

"Of course."

"One thing, though, don't try to get between a knife and me heroically. My Dragon skin is tougher than yours. Clear?"

"Oh. No?"

"Moreover, Francine and I are faster than you with these suits."

"I'm not as good as a Dragon, but I can surely keep up with her."

"Fatima. You don't know all the facts. This information is top secret. Francine is a bio-technically modified Mamba. She's better than you in every way."

Francine placed one hand on her shoulder. "I didn't volunteer to be trained as a Cartel killing machine. They simply seized us and put us on their program. That was before Jo came. She gave me and the other Mambas a choice. Now I protect her, but I kept my upgrades."

"Upgrades. Mmm. It sounds like I can't compensate for that by training harder."

"No. I can't tell you whose training was better, yours or mine. I can only tell you that I was highly motivated to be good, since girls who weren't good enough were eliminated."

CHAPTER THIRTY-ONE

Fatima was still digesting Francine's last remark when we approached the small crowd before the warehouse.

We had a little advantage. There were about twenty men standing under lights mounted on the warehouse roof when we came out of the dark. Even if they'd noticed our taxi, there was no way for them to know whether the driver had just withdrawn or unloaded passengers.

They noticed us when we reached the lit area's boundary. Their reaction to our arrival came in the form of numerous approving whistles and cheers.

Two of the men were bold enough to try to chat us up. One had his black hair tied in a long pigtail. The other one had stubble. Both were poorly shaved and wore wide-cut worker trousers and tank tops. Both smelled like beer and man.

Pigtail was obviously targeting Francine, while Stubble went for Fatima. So far, nobody had me on his radar.

"Hello, my sugar babe," Pigtail said. "Did you lose your way?"

"I'm not your sugar babe," Francine said and looked at his crotch. "At least not yet. Give way. I'm thirsty."

He tossed his almost-empty can aside and reached for her.

The next moment, he was lying flat on the ground, and Francine was standing above him as if she hadn't moved at all. Stubble paused and stared at her while Fatima was still preparing to deflect him.

Despite his opportunistic position, Pigtail was too dizzy to enjoy the view between Francine's legs.

"You want trouble?" Stubble said.

I passed my two companions. "No, Stubble. We want to have a beer and meet nice guys—guys who'll respect us, as we respect you."

"Look, the short one has a big mouth. Where do you think you've come?"

"Planet Earth, Australian continent, Queensland, Brisbane, Riverdowns, my waterhole of choice. You're right, though. I have a big mouth. I also have big tits and a huge thirst for beer. As long as the latter isn't quenched, the former aren't available. Clear? However, I'm ready to drink any of you under the table, defeat any of you at arm wrestling, or both. Who's first?"

Stubble began to grin. "What's the prize?"

"Me."

"You're just a half pint."

"Okay. The winner can have all three of us, in sequence or together. Normal, doggy or blowjob. He can enjoy us after sobering down."

Now he folded his arms and squinted. "And you said, you'll go against each of us?"

"That's my challenge. I only have two restrictions. This offer only lasts until sunrise, and I get time to pee after every two challengers."

"That looks like a clear result."

"You wish, Stubble. But tell me, what are your stakes?"

"What do you mean by that?"

"Hey, I'm betting my body and those of my friends. What do you bet? I mean, at least our drinks are on you. And . . ." I pretended to ponder. "If I persevere, it's my choice."

"Choice?"

"I get to choose challengers who will do us as *we* want it."

He looked around at his mates. It looked like a unanimous agreement to me. From their point of view, they just couldn't lose. I agreed. There'd be six winners, either way, three of us and three of them. Only the bill would be high.

Stubble raised a hand. "Uh, one more question."

"Yes, Stubble?"

"Schnapps or beer?"

"I don't care. I already said I'm thirsty. If you want schnapps, I'll drink it along with the beer."

He frowned. Had the blood from his cock found its way back to his brain? "Girl, something's fishy here. What kind of game are you playing?"

One of his mates stepped forward from the group and held his illuminated hand up to Stubble. I couldn't see the image projected on the palm, but that wasn't necessary. I could imagine what it was showing.

"You?" Stubble asked.

I shrugged and smiled.

"Ey, what's up?" one of the others asked.

The mate raised his illuminated hand. "It's her. Paladin Johanna."

"The Dragon empress?"

"The Protectress?"

"The Meier?"

"Paladin?"

"The University . . ."

"Velvet."

"Doesn't look like on TV."

"Man, what a pity!"

"Damn, those tits."

The comments echoed all around.

"I can't deny it," I said aloud. "Yes, I'm Jo."

Next, Stubble and Lighthand went down on their knees before me and lowered their heads, and the other men followed suit—except for Pigtail, who was still lying flat.

"Pardon me, Paladin. I didn't recognize you right away."

Stubble's voice trembled, and his eyes were gleaming wet when he looked up at me. "We—we're a bit rough here."

"Stand up, Stubble. Stand up, all of you. We know what kind of neighborhood this is. We're here for fun, and we can take a thumping."

He obeyed and slowly rose. "But you're . . ."

"A human like you. I'm entitled to earn respect like any other. Well. Now, I should say we can talk on eye level, but for that, I'd need a crate to stand on."

The laughter was on my side.

"Okay, guys." I pointed to my side. "This is Francine, my pilot. And Fatima, commandant of an armor suits infantry. How are things now? Do we get a beer?"

Lighthand glanced from Francine to Fatima. "*Knight* Francine? Ahm—armor suit doesn't tell me anything?"

What else might he know, then?

Fatima helped him out. "I follow Stormy Sylvie's example."

With raised brows, he glanced at her again. "In the foremost ranks? Hats off."

So he knew more than just the name of the first armor infantry company's leader, who had successfully defended Houston against several ten-thousand interstellar invaders.

We had successfully twisted these rough guys around our little fingers. The situation was looking cozy, when one of the men in the rear called out, "Hey! The Zombies are coming!"

He pointed at the far corner of the warehouse. Two dozen young men with leather jackets, baseball bats, chain sticks, knives, and bicycle chains were marching toward us. Their faces were painted red and white. The scene reminded me of New York and my visit to the Bronx.

Chapter Thirty-Two

My first concern was Stubble and his friends' safety. "Stay behind us. This is not your fight."

Despite his noticeable relief, he disagreed. "It should be our fight."

"Not today." Not with a Dragon *Protectress* present.

Before I could step toward the newcomers, though, Francine placed a hand on my arm. "My job."

Fatima gave me a questioning glance, but I only smiled in agreement. Francine was quite capable of handling this situation and — other than Stubble's group — these new brawlers didn't deserve the indulgence in my eyes.

No, Jo. Even these people belong to the protected. My *Analogy* was right, of course.

"Be gentle."

Francine nodded and smiled. "Naturally."

She elegantly walked toward the Zombies, balancing on her high-heeled shoes. Just like me, she immediately recognized the leader based on their formation, a tall blond with gloves and a butterfly knife.

"Hey, Blondie."

"Down with that dress," the leader demanded. "Reveal yourself if you wanna live."

Francine obediently lifted her left arm and reached for the zipper with her right. Then she slipped out of the strap on her shoulder. She took her time letting the dress slide over her body to the ground. Some of the men whistled. When her strip show ended, she stepped out of the dress pooled at her feet and *exploded*.

A few moments later, the twenty-four men were writhing on the ground in pain. Francine leaned over the leader and held his knife up to his crotch.

Fatima slowly let out her breath. "What was that?" she whispered.

"The upgrade. Francine is *fast*."

"What did you just say?" Francine asked her victim.

The Zombie leader saw the naked woman above him, heard his friends' moaning and whining and felt the steel's sharp coldness slowly penetrate his pants. "What?"

"Did you just threaten to take my life?"

"What—but, no—"

I could see her blade's pressure increase as her victim's tension grew.

"Yes. Okay, I threatened you. Please!"

Francine didn't reduce the pressure. "You will never again touch a knife. And I don't want to meet any of you ever again in a similar situation. Not in Brisbane, and nowhere else in Australia. Understood?"

"Yes. Yes! Who—what are you?"

"The woman with the knife at your balls. Now get lost."

Francine rose and took a step back. Dressed only in her high heels and holding the Zombie leader's knife, Francine watched the Zombies withdraw.

One tried to reach for his lost knife, then glanced at her. She slightly shook her head, and he made up his mind to run away as fast as he could without his weapon.

Once they all disappeared, Francine tossed the knife away, took her dress, dusted it, and put it on again.

"What a woman!" Stubble whispered behind me. "Damn, what I would give for . . ."

"Start with a beer," I cut him off before he could finish his thought.

CHAPTER THIRTY-THREE

A few steps before reaching the door, we got our first taste of what to expect inside. An intense mix of stale air, alcohol, male sweat, and farts, against which the overstrained air conditioner fought a losing battle, hit us. Francine took the lead by entering the warehouse first. I went in last.

Only about a quarter of the warehouse served as a bar at the right side of the warehouse. A wired fence that was two meters high separated the rest of the space. Crammed into the enclosed area were all kinds of old machines. In the shadows between the machines, I could spot the movements of small rodents and even smaller arthropods.

Compared with the dimly lit street outside, the bar area was bright. I could recognize the different bottle labels behind the counter to my right even without my enhancements. I read through them briefly.

My *Analogy* counted one hundred and four men assembled around a dozen beer barrels. Two young girls and three men behind the counter tended to their provisions.

The men showed us the way quietly and with respect. I heard no lewd remarks or whistles. The reason soon became apparent. A large screen above the door showed an image of the street, including the place where Francine disarmed and discouraged the Zombies.

Of course, their interested gazes followed us in. I could almost hear the wheels turning in their heads. Who were these three attractive, dangerous young women who so blatantly didn't fit in these surroundings?

We reached the counter unmolested. Finally!

"Everything's on me!" Stubble yelled behind us, his voice fighting to be heard above the rock music playing in the background.

"Three Fourex," Francine ordered before the bulky blond behind the counter could ask.

"Hello, beauty." A scrawny man with full beard addressed Fatima. "How comes Willy invited you for a beer? He hasn't done that since the Invasion."

She stopped and scrutinized him. "And who are you?"

"John. Although . . . you don't ask for names here. That's impolite. You come here to be anonymous."

"Oh, that's good. Sorry, John. I'll forget your name right away."

"No, it's okay. If you're told a name, you may use it. Well . . ."

"You may call me Fatima, John." She took two glasses of beer from Francine and gave me one. "I guess we impressed Willy."

"Ey, can you see anything from down there at all?" another bloke asked me from the side.

I left Fatima to her conversation partner and turned to the well-fed man in flap trousers. "Well, you can't be missed. But you're right. The view's limited. Hold that." I gave him my beer. Then I pointed at two glasses on the barrel next to him. "Would you take these away, please?"

The glasses disappeared. I turned my back to the barrel, pushed myself up and sat on the edge. If Ernesto knew about the dirt my butt was pressing his creation into, he'd probably faint, but my nanos were already busy cleaning the fabric covering my bum. I'd leave the barrel spotless and as good as new, once I was done here.

The men around me didn't fail to notice my transparent my dress or my physique underneath it. I pushed Flaptrousers' chin up before I took my glass of beer back.

"Hello, folks. I'm Jo. Is it always this gloomy here? Cheers! Cheers, Willy!"

Willy nodded at me. Then he focused his attention back on Francine.

Flaptrousers saluted at me, too. "Well, we're all still a bit speechless from your friend's performance out there. Nobody challenges the Zombies. When they return . . ."

"Francine will cut their balls off."

"I'd be cautious there. They don't like it when they're not taken seriously."

"Nor do we. But now they're gone. We're here, and I want to have some fun. Any takers?"

"Uh. Fun?"

I rolled my eyes. Then I finished my beer and gave it to Flaptrousers. "Refill that."

"Uh."

I briefly supported myself with both hands on the barrel, pulled my legs tight, and stood on the barrel. The surrounding men looked up at me with blank faces.

Then I began to dance very slowly.

CHAPTER THIRTY-FOUR

Fatima paused at the hotel restaurant door and told the young lady at the entrance her room number. While the latter checked her list, Fatima spotted us and sat next to us on the bench.

"Coffee?" I asked and held up a small pitcher.

"Yes, please." Her voice trembled slightly.

Francine and I patiently waited until she finished drinking her first sips. "You had a long night?"

Fatima smiled. "It was a long night." She glanced back and forth between us. "Where did you get those?"

We both wore matching white sweatshirts, comfy jogging pants, and plain flip-flops. Fatima was dressed in her uniform again.

"They're compliments of the house," Francine explained. "For guests who want to visit the fitness area or for those who arrived entirely without luggage."

"For two hours of sleep, you look astonishingly fit."

"Thanks, so do you. Did you survive?"

Fatima shrugged. "The muscles in my legs ache. It was, uh, different."

I tapped the pitcher in my hand. She nodded and held her cup up for me to fill.

"It was not what I expected. I thought we'd be addressed by the men, and after an appropriate amount of time, they'd take us—separately, one for each of us—somewhere private. There we'd have intercourse together."

"Yes, I thought along the same line," Francine said.

"Then Jo climbed the barrel. *Good,* I thought. *She'll tell the men something about the incident outside.* Instead, she moved her body."

"And *how* she moved her body." Francine glanced at me. I smiled apologetically.

"Yes, exactly. Okay, it pleased the men, but I thought it was just because of the dress. Then I began to tingle inside." Fatima hesitated. "When I think about it, I feel hot again. Before I knew it, I became so awake down there, you know?"

We both nodded.

"When I watched, it was a bit like I heard music, so I swayed with the rhythm in my head. The fabric of my dress caressed me down there while I moved, which only made me feel hotter down there."

I could imagine that. Fatima's clitoris significantly grew when excited, and it showed under the thin fabric as clearly as her hard nipples.

"She was dripping," Francine added. "At first, the guys around didn't notice. Then the guy next to me couldn't hold it any longer and took his cock out. He didn't care at all whether we were watching him jerk off."

"But you cared," I said.

"But I cared. I just had to wrap my right leg around his hip, and his cock slipped inside almost on its own."

She winked at Fatima. "In any case, my victim's mate watched us with envy, so I winked at him. Then I looked at Fatima and the puddle between her legs. He understood and showed her his boner."

"I was shocked," Fatima admitted. "I mean, we were in public, right? But the guy already had his hands on my ass and pulled my dress up to my hips. Of course, he immediately found out I wasn't wearing anything under it, so he assumed I wanted sex and simply took me."

"You could've said *No,*" I said.

Fatima didn't evade my gaze. "No, I couldn't. Well, yes. Okay. I was allowed to say *No*. I could have gone out of his reach. I could have kicked his privates. But I didn't *want* to do any of those things. I couldn't not want sex. Later he held my hips and lifted me up. Then he was inside me. At that moment, it felt incredibly good. I had no choice but to wrap my legs around him and join the rhythm."

Francine glanced at me as if she were saying we'd successfully corrupted her.

"I think I reached climax six or seven times last night," Fatima happily went on with her story. "I didn't know it could feel so good!"

I'd kept an eye on her last night to intervene if necessary. But the men didn't treat her too hard. They didn't force her to do things she wasn't ready to do, either. All they did was demonstrate how much more comfortable it could be to be taken from behind by a man. So I knew she didn't have an orgasm with every bloke.

"Eleven." Francine grinned lasciviously.

"With how many guys?" I asked.

"Twenty-five or thirty."

My pilot's quota was worse, but that was because she counted the cocks she had sucked, like me. We would never have been able to fuck all those men in such a short time. Well, all interested men. At least two dozen of them had sex with each other. That had hurt me a little. I'm used to making *all* men want me, even the gay ones. This time, I didn't manage to lure them all to me.

"And what are we doing tonight?" Fatima asked.

"Working."

"Oh, bummer."

I rose. "I don't want to make your father wait any longer. Just stay here. You haven't eaten yet."

PART FIVE—WORRIES

CHAPTER THIRTY-FIVE

Rashid's secretary came to me from the conference room door. He gave me a friendly nod and hurried on. I entered and closed the door behind me.

The Sheikh was pouring a cup of tea.

"Good morning, Johanna. Would you like some tea, too?"

"Gladly." I didn't really need the tea, but the gesture.

He poured tea into a second cup. "How are you?"

"Great. All day yesterday, nobody shot at me."

He laughed. "That's one way of judging it, too. And the evening?"

"It was very fulfilling. And yours?"

Rashid sat down in one of the chairs next to the table. I sat in the second one.

"I've tested the waters in the UN concerning your proposal. The Australians support you wholeheartedly, which surely doesn't surprise you. The American ambassador wasn't surprised and will pass your wish on to his president. As for the Russians and the Chinese, I didn't want to talk to them about it, yet. What's that saying? That's a very hot potato you handed me there."

"When you get close to a Dragoness, it can easily get hot."

"And if you can't stand the heat, don't come close. That's clear. I won't complain. But what's the other saying? Rome wasn't built in a day. I just need some more time."

"That's okay. I don't need the answer tomorrow. I only expect you to tell me if you can't get that topic taken care of. If your diplomatic channels don't work, we'll try mine."

"You have diplomatic contacts, too?" Smiling, he leaned forward and reached for his teacup.

"I could publicly announce that — in the long run — we can only keep the University open to students from countries that support the Dragon way."

His hand stopped short of his teacup's handle. "That's what you're calling diplomacy?"

"Dragon diplomacy. Precise, logical, straightforward. Always right on the bullseye." I smiled and picked up my teacup. "As we often only work with insinuation in human diplomacy, you might be able to use insinuation in this direction as leverage — now that you know how far I'm willing to go."

Rashid smiled back. "You're a dangerous woman."

I didn't have to comment on that. I drank my tea, and another idea came to my mind. "The Russians and the Chinese tried in vain to gain advantages in their applications to the University."

I reported the course of our negotiations.

In the end, he nodded. "I understand. So it could be that they'd like to get back at you now."

"I want to be fair. All have the same chance. That's Dragon policy. But this rule only applies as long as the community is based on mutual solidarity."

"Yes. I will try to explain your position."

"I don't have positions. I have a goal. My goal is to prepare Earth for a new invasion in the best possible way. To reach this goal, I must utilize my resources wisely. To control this utilization, I need influence in the respective boards." I shrugged. "As I said yesterday, we must be clear about the foundation of our collaboration. We must clearly define the chain of command, reporting lines, competencies, and responsibilities. Negotiating these topics will take time — perhaps a lot of time — and we will make good use of this time to create facts that can't be negotiated away later. So, let's talk about your questions now. Yesterday you mentioned two big topics?"

"Yes. I'm worried about this incident in the desert."

Chapter Thirty-six

"All remnants of this strange organism were burnt. Any wreckage is headed toward the sun and will be annihilated there. The wormhole has collapsed, so no danger threatens us from there either, right?" the Sheikh summed up.

"Correct."

Rashid sighed. "So we're cut off for now, are we?"

"Why? What are you thinking?"

"I'm wondering where this last invader originated."

"We know that," I admitted. Perhaps I should have said, *we will know that,* as this information had to be available in our data. We only had to filter it out.

"Wherever it came from, there could be more of this plague."

"Not our problem." Not while I had so many more urgent issues on my mind.

"Not yet, right. Once the second wave reaches our galaxy, it also comes *there*. Then the plague could manage to capture another Jelly spaceship. I don't think it will help us to ignore this problem. It's just that as long as we can't travel to the pest's home planet, we have no means of destroying it or preventing its expansion."

"Now I understand." He was right. I had learned the hard way what it meant to ignore problems until they came knocking at your door. "Who says we can't travel there?"

"We don't have such a spaceship."

"No. But we know how a wormhole generator works. We observed the entire creation phase and now know which

110

effects must be caused. We have the construction blueprint from the spaceship the Lionhearts used to depart our planet. We can build a wormhole generator."

"Great! Only, I seem to hear a *but* coming."

"Yes, Rashid. I don't think our economy can afford to build and equip a spaceship that is fifty kilometers big. I'd like to build a smaller wormhole generator that fits into a significantly smaller spaceship."

"Then, do that."

"For that, I'd practically have to start from scratch. The aggregates the Jellies use to create wormholes are incredibly crude. I don't know whether it pays to refine them, or whether we should build something new. I'd like some time to think about that."

"Well, we aren't talking about a project that should start next week. We must lay the foundation for it first. We must be able to defend ourselves before we open a two-way path."

I nodded. "I agree with this prioritization, but the project must start soon. We need a military strategy and a scientific plan for exploration, and the University can't do that. We must get smart brains from across the globe to work on this topic."

"You already have ideas?"

"Only whatever surfaces. We must ask clear questions first, like what exactly are we looking for, or what should an interstellar expedition achieve? I assume we must keep a strict quarantine. Whatever gets in contact with that substance may not return to our solar system."

"Oh. Of course."

"After all, we don't want to bring new problems home. As long as we don't know what tricks the enemy has up his sleeves, we basically may not allow any return at all, since even interstellar dust might be contaminated. Moreover, neither this opponent nor any other parties may gain access to a new wormhole generator. That means we may not even send a spaceship with such a generator through the wormhole we create. It needs to be a one-way street."

"That would be a suicide mission. Who'd volunteer for such a thing?" Rashid looked at me. "Oh no. We couldn't accept such a sacrifice. Besides, if no one returns, we won't gain new findings. What would be the point in such a mission?"

That made me smile. "Right. We need to think about this mission thoroughly, so we should start planning immediately."

"Good." He folded his hands. "Then I have no more questions for today. Oh, and one more thing, my daughter formally submitted her application to transfer to the United Nations forces."

CHAPTER THIRTY-SEVEN

I met up with Francine at the restaurant exit. "Are we leaving?" she asked.

"Yes. There's a lot to do."

"Okay." She pointed at the elevator. "What about our stuff?"

"We can have it shipped to us."

"How about my suit?"

"Okay, you're right." Her protective suit was too expensive, so I followed her. "It's probably better if we leave by the roof."

"I don't think so. Unless you want to show the press you fear them."

"Oh. Thanks for the tip."

"You're welcome."

An elevator's door opened for us, and we slipped inside before it could close. Francine pressed our floor number.

"Fatima's a rebel," she said.

"What do you mean? Did she say that?"

"I read it between the lines. She rebels against her religion's traditional gender roles, where women have nothing to say. She claims the same rights and liberties as a man. Promiscuity is part of that. I don't think she really liked the gang bang last night. Okay, she came, so it wasn't entirely off. She didn't like the sex in itself, though. She liked the feeling of being able to have sex."

"So what? I feel the same."

"Right. Me, too. She wants to be like you, Jo, free like you."

"Okay. I won't begrudge her that."

Francine pouted. "Jo, she's an officer, not a Dragon. She will lead a military unit in a disciplined way."

"Yes, and? To me, it seems she's doing fine there so far."

"Naturally. She must strictly maintain the role of a stern officer to be taken seriously as a woman and to get ahead in her career. She's playing the conformer because she's smart, and is even deceiving her father. But can she keep that up and at the same time follow you?"

I didn't particularly like the way our conversation was heading. The elevator stopped at our floor, and we walked to our room. When we were in front of the door, Francine continued the conversation. "She stripped to the buff before her father without timidity or hesitation, and she's surely not a die-hard nudist. Why?"

"To show her strong will and obedience?"

"Yes, sure. But it's not about the fact that she stripped, but the way she stripped. Consider that."

She gave me time to remember the scene, opened the room door, and let me enter first.

"She was a bit embarrassed."

"Yes. But not more than a bit. She glanced at her father repeatedly. You noticed that, didn't you? You gave her the perfect reason to deliver the ultimate provocation, public nudity."

"It wasn't entirely public."

"It was before strangers. She didn't know us, and he didn't know us yet, either. Considering her cultural background, that's extreme." She took off her sweatshirt. "Don't get me wrong, your rationale was right. She'll have to do it again. Only I think she did it for the wrong reasons."

"And?"

"And that's a bad place to start." She sat down on the bed to remove pants and flip-flops. "Whatever she does, must be grounded on the right reasons."

"What do you propose? Shall I talk her out of having sex?"

"I think it's too late for that."

"Or should I be a better role model from now on, that is, do without acts like yesterday?"

"You've sacrificed enough."

"Then I don't have a solution now."

"No, neither do I." She sighed and began to put on her suit. "Moreover, I fear that could become fodder for religious zealots. Imagine the headlines. *Dragon empress seduces demure officer to be immoral,* or something like that."

"If you put it like that . . . Damn, I should have thought of that."

"Jo, I'm sorry. I didn't want to give you a bad conscience. I just think we should watch how it evolves."

"Yes. We should." I watched the seams of her nano suit close automatically.

"I'm ready. What about you?"

"Me? Oh." In a hurry, I dropped my comfy clothes and let my nanos form the black combat suit. "Ready."

"Really? Even for the press?"

"Oh. Wait." I added my belt and skull buckle and put on the order's brooch. "Now I'm ready."

CHAPTER THIRTY-EIGHT

All eyes turned toward us when we appeared in the hotel lobby. Guests stopped in their tracks, while hotel staff paused their work. Only two young men jumped up and dared to approach us.

One quickly reached into his bag, as the pair closed in on us. Francine's whole body tensed up until she saw the man pull out a camera from his bag. Without consultation, she left the two obvious targets to me and focused on the rest of the lobby.

"Protectress, can you spare a moment of your time for us?" the first man asked. He wore a polo shirt, Bermuda shorts, and canvas shoes. Judging by his beard stubble and the wrinkles on his shirt, he had spent all night in the lobby.

His partner was similarly dressed, including the wrinkled shirt. The only difference was that the second man wore long trousers instead of Bermuda shorts. He was still fighting with his gear when they reached me.

"Of course, gladly. But please let your friend change the battery without haste. I won't run away."

He smiled, and both men visibly relaxed.

"What's your name?"

"Josh. Josh Paul. My mate with the camera is Matt Dixon. We work for Oz Streaming."

Eventually the new battery clicked into place. Matt switched the camera on, checked the display, and gave us a thumbs-up.

I smiled at Josh and waited. He smiled back at me.

"Josh Paul for Oz Streaming. We met the Protectress Johanna Meier while she was leaving her hotel here in Brisbane. Protectress Johanna, you only returned to Earth a week ago. How do you feel?"

"I'm relieved because of our victory. I'm glad all my companions survived. I still shake when I think of how we barely managed to build a rudimentary defense."

"There are already numerous comments concerning your last point. Can you give us your opinion on them?"

"No, Josh. I haven't heard any of the comments you mentioned. I haven't found time to read commentaries or even do a comprehensive debriefing with my team since my return."

"How come? Did the battle bother you so much?"

"I didn't have time to be bothered, either, Josh. First, we had to make sure that this attack wave was truly over — which is true, but we wanted to rule out any risk. Immediately afterward, I talked with the UN Secretary for Interstellar Defence about our next steps. The events showed us that we mustn't lose time in preparing Earth for the next invasion."

"That was a subject in many of the commentaries I mentioned. Wasn't the recent attack the last wave? The Lionheart had only talked about two waves."

Okay. The grace period is over. "Josh, this was on no account the second wave. This was an irregular attack."

"But it was a Jelly mothership?"

"Yes, that's correct. We must assume that we humans aren't the only ones who can capture a Jelly mothership, and that other enemies of the Jellies aren't automatically our friends. We can't pinpoint the reasons for the recent attack, but we *can* tell that it was atypical."

"We only know of one Jelly invasion so far. How can you draw conclusions from that?"

I nodded at Josh. "That's the right question, Josh, and the wrong premise. You are correct in saying that we've only experienced one invasion thus far. However, a rough first analysis told us that the recent invasion was not typical. The good news is that the same Dragon technology that warned us about the recent attack—that allowed us to equip our prototypes in time and get them into space—also offers us the opportunity to detect the echoes of wormholes, that is, of other interstellar travels." "

He needed a moment to digest this statement. "We can detect other interstellar travels?"

Josh asked too many closed-ended questions. Until now I'd let it slide, but I wouldn't make it too easy for him. "Yes."

"Using Dragon technology?"

"Yes."

As I gave him no lead for further questions and he didn't seem to have any idea how to dig deeper into this subject, he asked a standard question next.

"Protectress Johanna, what was the reason for your visit in Brisbane?"

"I was here for a first extensive conversation with the UN Secretary for Interstellar Defence."

"And what was the subject of this conversation?"

"Well, we had to get to know each other first, so we talked about the distribution of duties and how we could collaborate. The Dragon way is significantly different from the customs of military personnel and politicians, so we had to find common ground. We identified areas of work that require research as well as preparations. For the time being, I'll mainly concentrate on research."

"What areas of research exactly?"

"Of course, it's about analyzing our recorded data, but we also have to process the experience from our first space mission and develop ideas on how to improve the crews' chances of survival. This time, we improvised and were very lucky, but I don't want to rely on luck alone."

"Understandable. You and the UN Secretary didn't only talk about experiences though. You mentioned that you two talked about preparations. What kind of preparations?"

"I don't know what's been publicly announced so far, and I don't want to anticipate the official statements, but you may assume that our defense against the second invasion won't rely on two experimental fighters and one spaceship alone. We talked about that."

"So it was about building additional forces?"

"That's a plausible conclusion, Josh. Our experience with the first wave suggests the units we'll need. So I don't need to say anything about that. My task is to consider whether there are practical applications of the Meier effect that could help us."

"What would those be?"

"Oh please, Josh. Your followers are very welcome to come up with their own ideas, as I need some more time to sort out my thoughts. That's the cue, by the way, Josh. You can ask one last question."

He briefly thought about what I just said. "Okay. Protectress Johanna. Why does most of your team seem to be female? Are women better fighters in space? Or is that owed to your personal criteria?"

Francine's face turned grim when she heard the last question—luckily outside the camera's view.

"Josh, with regard to my personal preferences, you're poorly informed. Your observation regarding my team is correct, though. Many of them are women. However, the reason isn't that I prefer to hire women, but that I have chosen to primarily save women from men who do bad things to them. You can hardly blame me for that. Nor can you blame those women for following me. I find tasks for them that match their qualifications."

"Without looking for other suitable candidates first?"

119

"Yes, Josh. From the moment our first readings warned us about unwanted visitors in space heading toward Earth, we had only three weeks to train our first pilots and send them to space. Would you feel better if we had asked for applications first?"

He stepped away from me.

"Probably not. You'd be long dead by now, or you'd be glad if you were allowed to die. Think about it. Goodbye, Josh, Matt."

Chapter Thirty-nine

Francine lolled into the backseat of the minivan and grinned up at me. "You finished him off nicely."

I placed one arm over the back rest of my seat and peeked over it. "He wasn't prepared well. Or perhaps he was, but he hadn't slept well and didn't remember all his questions. So he had to pull something out a hat."

"Insinuating that you had *personal criteria* when selecting your team was mean."

"Oh, that was just poorly phrased. I've had worse questions before."

"Please buckle up," the driver called from the front.

I had planned to take a taxi, but a minivan with tinted windows was already waiting for us at the front of the hotel. Had Rashid or the hotel organized this ride for us?

I didn't need a belt, but I didn't want to cause the driver trouble, so I sat down straight and buckled my seat belt.

The fabric felt hard and stiff. I hadn't used a seat belt in years, but this one felt different. I didn't let it click into place. "Stop," I told Francine, who was still pulling at her own belt.

My nanos were already analyzing its fabric and the buckle. The belts were reinforced with metal threads. I gave the windows a closer look, too. They were thicker than normal.

Not on my watch. I sent a nano thread to the engine.

The driver held his breath and leaned forward.

Before his finger could reach the nondescript button on the dashboard, I had reached his seat, grabbed his shoulder, and pulled it back. "Hands off!" I commanded.

He tried to surprise me by stepping firmly on the pedal, but my nano wire reached the power controller and intercepted the drive current.

The sudden deceleration could have thrown him forward against the button, but I held his shoulder in an iron grip.

Francine tried in vain to open the sliding door. It didn't surprise me that it was locked. I retrieved my first thread and sent a second to eat the bolt in the lock.

"Again."

Francine pulled the handle, and this time, the sliding door opened. After a glance at the street and the next houses, she exited. "Okay."

"I will leave now," I told our driver. "Don't follow me, and tell your folks they shouldn't try another stunt like this. I won't be as forgiving again."

In a single motion, I let him go and left the minivan. I nodded at Francine and pointed in the general direction of the airport.

"You're not worried that he'll shoot?" she asked.

"He was supposed to capture us alive."

"For what?"

"I guess the unknown party, the people who hired him. They probably want to talk with me. I do, too, but not this way."

"And now?"

"Over there." I pointed at a smaller hotel two blocks away. "We'll surely find a taxi there."

CHAPTER FORTY

The screen showed a green blot with a narrow white edge, surrounded by a brown-speckled light blue area, inside a dark blue body of water—Velvet Island. We could see the familiar green trees, white sand of our home island, even the corals in the shallow water inside the reef. More coral reefs, some enclosing smaller islands, surrounded Velvet Island and decorated the Pacific Ocean.

"It's so nice here," Sylvie noted. "We have to do such ugly things sometimes. Velvet Island reminds us what we are fighting for every day. It's good to see it again, isn't it?"

The former Mamba was leaning on my Companion, holding onto him tightly. Was she talking of her fellow Mambas' duties, or just her own? How deep did the terror of her near-death experience in space affect her? Did she feel like I did after my Taipan dissolved? I was all alone in that horrible accident, without a Dragon protectively wrapping himself around me, but I at least had been able to see our blue planet.

Her gaze met mine, and she smiled, embarrassed. "Jo, I . . ."

Sylvie looked up to Achrotzyber. "It's . . ."

Then she lowered her head again. "You . . ."

"You don't have to explain anything," I said in a friendly voice.

"But I must. It's . . . difficult."

My first impulse was to object. But she was right. "Of course it is. I can hardly understand how you feel. It was lonely, wasn't it?"

"I . . . I still don't entirely grasp it."

"No. You don't have to. But he was there for you."

"Yes."

"He was the only one who could help you. It's entirely natural that you stick to him. Achrotzyber *protects* you. I'd have done the same with Francine." Our pilot briefly looked up to me, smiled, then focused on landing the spacecraft again.

"But . . ."

"Just as naturally, he couldn't just leave you alone once we were back on Earth. You still needed him, perhaps still need him."

"Yes . . ." She pulled him a bit tighter. "He's your Companion."

"That's right." I watched my Dragon Companion's athletic human shape and felt warm inside.

Companion? he asked in my head.

Later.

She briefly glanced at Francine, then back at me. "He . . . he not only held me."

"I know, Sylvie. That's okay."

"No. Not with you and Achrotzyber. I know, we all take it easy on the island. But with you . . ."

"With us, it's different. We have a relationship that reaches beyond love and sex. In our relationship, it's not about owning but about sharing. We share our joy with each other and with others. When Achrotzyber gives you joy, I win, too. You see?"

"N-n-o."

"Your joy makes him happy, and his happiness, in turn, pleases me."

Not to mention the fact that he still needed to learn how to please women. It wasn't done with the technical act of penetration and a few shakes of the pelvis alone. Sylvie was a perfect first teacher, because she didn't have any big demands. All she wanted was to be close to someone.

"Once we've set down, we'll get something to drink from Nanette. Then we'll sit down on the beach, and I'll tell you what I learned about wellness and erotica, okay?"

Not that I'd stop at storytelling.

CHAPTER FORTY-ONE

"Ooooh!"

Sylvie pulled at my arms, wrapped her right arm around me, and held me tightly. I pushed some sand under my left arm away to rest more comfortably and arranged my right leg over her upper legs. After that, I placed my right hand around the base of her left breast. That way we remained reclining.

Now and then, a big wave lapped at our feet, but the ocean was receding. Soon the way to the coral reef wall would be safe to walk again.

I listened for telltale signs, but she didn't cry out this time. Her breath remained even.

This time, she'd been able to enjoy her orgasm. This time, she wasn't so shaken up that her body trembled and I had to hold her. This time, she held me.

My thoughts returned to the earlier evening.

Before exploring each other's bodies, I'd told her about my time in the brothel. I explained Eva Keller's philosophy to her and told her what it meant to submit to passion entirely and to be willing to give and receive joy. A quickie didn't have to be a contradiction when both lovers wanted it, and the same applied to caressing each other until climax.

During my little lecture, I sent subliminal messages — an open body position, an appropriate scent, an occasional touch — that helped her relax.

Her experience had distressed her more than she admitted to herself and us. She'd tried to be brave and acted like she

126

was over it, but I sensed how tense she felt — at least, before my treatment.

My first cunnilingus made her scream out loud in ecstasy with her orgasm, had made her body writhe and shake. Now, she was relaxed.

"So many stars," she whispered.

I remained silent.

"So many stars. Jo, I've always dreamt of stars. I wished I could fly up there one day. Now I can, and I don't want to lose that."

"You don't have to."

"But I'm afraid. I'm afraid of what could happen. I'm so scared that I would fail in a crucial moment due to my fear. I may not be able to keep pretending that nothing happened and put you all in danger. I must not fly another combat mission."

"Sylvie . . ."

"No, Jo. I need a good headshrinker, one who really knows his stuff. Your help today was good. I feel more at ease, but it's not enough. I need to find out what's going on with me, and until then . . ."

"Until then, we need a flight instructor with first-hand experience. We need pilots to build our remote stations and deliver provisions there. We need test pilots for our new toys. We have such a big demand for pilots that I don't know where to start. So, surely, there will be a place for you here that matches your dream."

I sensed her heart beating faster. "And, one day, when you feel ready to fly a warship again, you'll get one."

"Oh, Jo!"

CHAPTER FORTY-TWO

I must get out of here!
My head buzzed from trying to figure out how to create a more efficient yet less noisy nestle field, a greater range for our cake knife while increasing its aiming accuracy, how to improve our space suits and build more robust spaceships.

They were all correct. We had fought like two torpedo boats against a battleship. However, no one could deny that it was efficient regarding cost and tonnage. Two such small spaceships took out such a colossus and only lost one small spaceship. We couldn't afford to lose any of the few space pilots we had left, though. Plus, Reginald had rightly pointed out that humanity couldn't afford to lose the knowledge inside my head—not to mention the smart ideas that were occasionally escaping from there.

We couldn't afford to build battleships, either. So we'd need more torpedo boats that were better built, and expendable pilots—as brutal as that sounded, we couldn't deny it.

We'd need more disruptor torpedoes to arm the torpedo boats.

Aw damn, we needed more of everything—more heads, more hands, more steel, more production lines, more nanos, more, more, more. We needed more time, as well.

We had to learn more from our experiences. To do that we had to understand the readings from our mission and learn to draw conclusions. There were countless dissertations you could write on the different flavors of interaction between artificial and natural gravity fields alone.

Meanwhile, one pinboard no longer sufficed for our tasks. We had three now. We had one for the core team, consisting of our teachers and our older students, one for the younger students, and one for topics that could be *crowdsourced* on the internet. But there was no one to check and condense the feedback from the internet.

Besides that, we still had to teach our students something new, too. Without lectures, we'd never solve our personnel shortage problem.

There was something else.

"Thousand-fold cursed infernal crap!"

My yell caused all the discussions around me to fall mute. Everyone froze. Nanette abruptly paused while filling a glass of wine and spilled a large gush of good Australian Shiraz.

All eyes turned to me.

"Damn, damn, damn! Why didn't I think of gathering the other old Dragon technology graduates?" I asked furiously, at no one but myself.

Okay, the technical college on the mainland was underway and very popular, thus producing new graduates on a regular schedule, but I had entirely neglected the already graduated experts who hadn't gained freedom when the worldwide crime Cartel collapsed.

"You once said they might be unreliable," Tess argued. "I admit, I've forgotten about that topic, too."

I nodded toward the leader of our *Mambas*.

"Me too," I admitted. "We had a lot to do back then. We were in acute danger several times, and we couldn't afford to take the risk of them working for their own profit. Now, though, with all the things we want to do, we'll *have* to take that risk."

"We shouldn't rush into this," Tess said.

"I'll give you the last addresses from *Project Orchestra*. That was the Cartel's code name for their exclusive access to

Dragon technology experts and keeping them captive. We need a plan. We'll have to check whether the intel is up-to-date and whether or not we can still find these people. We needn't stir anyone up until we know for certain what we want from them and how to deal with them."

"Okay."

"I'm sorry," I said.

Tess only nodded.

"I need fresh air."

Then I walked out.

CHAPTER FORTY-THREE

I heard my Companion's steps following me in the sand. I smelled his light apple scent and subliminally sensed his signature's proximity.

"You only heard the end of the discussion," I said, gazing across the red golden wave patterns.

He didn't have to confirm my statement, so he pondered which question I might have connected with it. He had learned that much about human communications.

"At this early point, I can neither contribute to the cursory analysis nor the creative ideas. This process is mainly not about logic, but about the mutual adaptation of associative connections. My mental patterns are too strange and would thus have a rather disruptive effect."

I nodded.

"Companion, would you be willing to accompany me?"

"Sure. Where?"

"To the next island."

"Yes, why?"

He hesitated. Why didn't he want to tell me the reason? Did he want to have an unbiased assessment of something? Or was it something the others shouldn't hear?

"Forget it. Go head. I'll come along."

We circled the communication center. Numerous rotting leaves were scattered over the sandy path between the trees. The wind had even spread some of them on the helipad.

Once we reached the jetty, I dashed away. Achrotzyber followed, then I let him pass. At the jetty's end, we both catapulted ourselves forward to dive into the channel water with a long arc.

A school of orange-red fish scattered apart, while a startled small shark changed its course.

My nanos formed fins at my feet, webbed fingers, and nictitating membranes over my eyes. I decided not to grow gills for the short leg.

My Companion swam around our reef's western tip and turned north, seemingly confirming my guess on our destination. Later, he headed slightly more eastward.

There was another lengthy, reef-bordered island in that direction, only about thirteen kilometers away. As part of the national park, it was closed to visitors, as far as I knew.

Shortly before reaching the beach, Achrotzyber slowed down.

Please close your eyes.

Oh. What did this mean? *Okay.*

He took me in one arm and pulled me a little distance forward. Then I felt him carrying me onto shore.

I let my fins, webs, and membranes disappear. The salt water rolled off my body. His strong arms held me, and it filled me with joy. I felt like purring and wondered if he understood this emotional expression.

After a few steps on the dry, soft sand he placed me down. I felt a blanket. *Where did he conjure that up?*

I heard a scratching noise and smelled something burning. "You can open your eyes now."

When I opened my eyes, I saw one of our tablecloths draped over a solid board in the sand. I saw perfectly decorated cutlery and crockery on the tablecloth. Slender candles were burning in two silver holders. Their flames marvelously matched the setting sun's red-golden reflexes.

Achrotzyber fetched a bottle of sparkling wine from an esky next to the board and opened it easily. The drink sparkled in deep blackberry red as he poured it into a champagne glass.

He gave me one glass and raised the other toward me. "Cheers."

"Cheers." We clinked our glasses together and drank. *Ah!* The intensely fruity taste lingered in my mouth.

"It's wonderful, but why . . ."

"You needed a change. You had to get out of there. Most importantly though, we need a little time together, so that you understand not only with your mind but also with your heart that I am there for you. You need the emotional hold."

I had no clue what to say.

"Companion, I learned to know you as a very strong woman, but I also learned what happens when burdens become too heavy. The way tasks are befalling you these last couple of days—you put it like that, right? I feared it would soon become too much again. I considered what I could do and reached the conclusion that I must prescribe a pause to you."

"And then you planned this?" I pointed at the table.

He smiled, and I noticed that this smile marvelously matched his blond curls and dimple.

"I had help. I asked Nanette how a man can express his affection to a woman other than by physical love. It took great effort to prevent her from coming here and setting the table."

I had to grin when I imagined that. Yes, when it was about my well-being, Nanette was hard to stop.

CHAPTER FORTY-FOUR

My Companion placed a plate with a large brown ball, surrounded by berries, before me. "Mousse Au Chocolat with a variation of berries."

For a moment I pondered what it would be like if I sucked this chocolate mousse from a hard male member, but I discarded the idea. The effort my Companion had invested to treat me to this tasty pleasure deserved exclusive attention.

I waited until he sat before his plate. Then I took my spoon and sampled the dessert. *Oh yes.* It was as good as expected.

"Wonderful," I praised. "Now tell me one thing, how did you manage to serve the steak for the main course so hot? It tasted like it was freshly prepared."

"It was. Kurt had given some thought to applying nano technology so spaceships could have a compact kitchen. With a battery, the result is portable."

He pointed at the boxes next to the table. "The cooling unit runs on batteries, too. Would you like another glass of sparkling wine?"

"Always." I held up the glass so he could fill it. "Thank you. I really needed this."

"Naturally." He pondered. "Sylvie gave me the idea. She had very intense emotional needs. I considered whether you could have similar needs. It seemed logical. I watched you. Your tension could not be missed. Is it not a Companion's most important task to fulfill emotional needs among humans?"

"Yes, indeed."

"I admit that I was initially unsettled when I felt this irrational wish inside me to be close to you. Having an emotional need still feels unfamiliar to me. And . . ."

"Mighty," I interrupted him. "Stop talking about emotional needs. Are you trying to tell me that you found out what love is?"

He hesitated. "No. I want to tell you that I found out what it means to love you."

CHAPTER FORTY-FIVE

A single black-tipped reef shark slowly drifted along under the jetty, under my toes. I watched my Companion swim down the navigable channel toward the sea and wished I could follow him.

But I could spot Freddie's yacht on the horizon. I had decided to welcome our new guest personally. So I remained sitting on the jetty's edge, swinging my legs.

At least, here at the jetty's outer end, I could quietly muse about our first space mission's results. The most important result was Achrotzyber's discovery of his emotional world.

It was only four years ago that we'd met during a battle in front of the Japanese emperor's palace, when I'd waited for him to impale me with his sharp claw. He hadn't killed me, though. Instead the merely twenty-year-old Dragon—still a cub by our standard—found an unexpected soulmate in me, since I was the only other creature in this solar system commanding a *signature* – a Dragon's form of telepathy.

It had only been logical to make him my *Companion* — my life partner and co-ruler as unchallenged Dragon empress on this planet—so far. It had been a purely rational relationship until he finally found out how to assume human shape—and what a hot shape that was—and began to learn about human motivations and emotions. It had been a long journey for both of us, short on any human or Dragon timescale, but intense.

I had truly only thought of doing something good forSylvie when I had left her in the strong, capable arms of Achrotzyber and voluntarily decided not to interfere with their relationship. I had allowed my Companion to be her *Protector* and sex partner. I had expected to lose him to her for a longer time.

But since our return to the island, she no longer clung to him. Now, it seemed like she had a different inclination and regarded her time with my Companion as an episode.

During their time together, my strictly logical Companion gained a lot of insights about humans and emotions — most of all about female emotions, at least enough to touch my heart. What more could I ask for?

I could ask for the ability to brace myself and think of my scientific tasks and not my partner — and his big cock which he could handle so skillfully. *Oooh. Dammit, Jo. Not again!*

Freddie's yacht turned toward the channel. Since I had hired him and his yacht for a rescue mission to Kwajalein and back, he was our regular connection to the mainland. Also he refused to consider as much as a day off because he was engaged to Beate, another of our Mambas.

I rose and noted that my lubrication had already left a wet spot on the jetty's timber. It didn't matter.

Beate was standing at the railing, a rope in her hand. She didn't need to hide her evenly tanned body, like me, so our new guest had the time and opportunity to get accustomed to our dress code.

CHAPTER FORTY-SIX

He wore a white straw hat, a long-sleeved shirt, shorts, and sunglasses. He sported a blond beard as well. When I saw him, I concluded that he'd need more time to get used to our dress code.

The newcomer waited patiently, while Beate fastened the lines forward and aft. Then he jumped on the jetty and reached out his hand.

"Hello! I'm Peter Jorgenson. You must be Johanna Meier, right?"

At least he was barefoot. I took his hand. "Right. Hello, Peter. How was your journey?"

"Very long. I'm not used to the time difference yet — and even less to the sun. I guess once I take my shirt off, I'll have a capital sunburn within three minutes."

"Oh, we can do something about that. Come along now."

He turned back, and Beate waved at him. "Go ahead. We'll bring your luggage ashore together with the other freight."

"Okay. Thank you!" He turned back to face me. "I'm glad you invited me. The photos don't do this paradise justice."

"Why? Too shallow?"

"They miss *everything* — the fresh air, the ripple of the waves, the light, and, of course, the attractive locals."

I laughed. "No, the photos are carefully selected. We don't want to attract people for the wrong reasons."

Together, we ambled down the jetty. "Regarding the sun, we share that problem with the corals. They can't bear it infinitely either. But if you notice, the corals aren't sunburned.

138

You know why?"

"No."

"The algae living with and inside the corals produce a sunscreen. We synthesize this substance. If you take it regularly, you won't get sunburned, either."

"Ah. That makes life easier." He pulled at his shirt. "I beg your pardon for not having adapted yet."

"No, that's okay. Nobody demands that you undress."

"I thought that's common here?"

"Common is correct, only not because we demand it, but because nobody likes to do laundry here."

"Ah, okay. Very pragmatic."

"That is another a rule here. Always be pragmatic."

"Fine. Uh—I'm not used to nudism. How does one handle spontaneous reactions?"

"You mean spontaneous *erections*, Peter." I waved at one of the invisible guards. "You let it happen, show what you've got, and smile at the causer. We are not nudists, Peter. We simply welcome natural nakedness. An erection is quite normal, to suppress it isn't normal. It just happens. If it pleases the causer, she might make you a proposal. That's normal, too, as a boner counts more or less like an assent—or even as a proposal. So you shouldn't be surprised if you see couples in the act somewhere on the beach."

"Oh, hmm."

"You don't have to join them, Peter. You can, though, if you want."

We had reached the end of the jetty. I pointed at the path between the trees, and we continued our walk.

"In any case, I assume you can. We like some change occasionally, and we don't have visitors often."

"Doesn't that cause jealousy?"

"Rarely. We're all adult, intelligent people working for a joint goal. Of course, there are exclusive couples, but most have understood that it's not about ownership."

"That's not always easy."

"No. So far we've been spared any drama. But that's not why I invited you here."

"No. Does she know I've come?"

"Not yet. So far, nobody knows about you. I haven't found the time to mention it. You'll see why very soon."

"I'm curious."

While we were approaching the communication center, the noise from inside grew louder. As always during the last days, several discussions filled the building. Those who didn't want to disturb their fellow researchers at work came here and enjoyed Nanette's attentive service.

Peter followed me through the door into the roof-covered open-air room with a seaside view, but stopped after the first three steps.

Three groups of naked people had gathered in rattan chairs, between which Nanette hastily scurried around. All the groups were debating quietly, but fervently. At first, nobody took note of us. Only after delivering another tray of drinks did Nanette approach us.

"Hello! You're new here. Welcome to Velvet Island. I'm Nanette. I'm responsible for your physical well-being and all non-scientific questions. What would you like to drink?"

"Hello, Nanette. Erm — I'm Peter. A mineral water, please."

"Gladly. Where are you from? Sweden?"

"Almost right. Norway. But I've been working in New York recently."

"Norway — the country of fjords. I've only seen pictures. It must be beautiful, only cold. I'll be right back." She hurried away.

Peter watched her leave. He wouldn't become the first man who'd fail to give Nanette's bum proper attention. "Cold? I guess compared to here, Norway is cold."

"She's from the southern portion of France and is used to the Mediterranean climate."

"Ah, I see."

"Pick a seat. There's plenty free ones."

Peter chose the table that was farthest away from all the others and sat down. I took the opposite seat. Soon Nanette arrived with a bottle of mineral water, a chilled glass, and a beer for me.

Peter thanked her. His gaze followed Nanette back to the counter. Only after she disappeared behind it did he pour himself water and glance at me.

I smiled at him. "She's really cute, isn't she?"

"And surely taken?"

"She's with François. He handles our suppliers, so he's often away. When he's here, she belongs to him. When he isn't, well, let's just say she's very affectionate."

"Really?" Suddenly he was very alert.

"Did I awaken your professional interest? Many of the women working for me had bad experiences in their former lives—before I freed them. Nanette is not an exception. She was looking for a steady relationship, but only had affairs—nothing truly horrendous. Now she's in a steady relationship and a place she feels needed, safe, and secure."

"What's something truly bad for you?"

"Daily systematic torture and rape for months."

Peter drank two glasses of water, and when Nanette brought my second beer, he pointed at it. Only after he had taken a long draft of his beer did he continue talking. "I didn't expect to find such big problems here."

"I didn't ask you to come here for them. Our girls get along quite well."

"Really? Sometimes the problems are hidden deep inside."

"That's your expertise. They seem fine to me. Perhaps they

don't want to appear weak, but we don't have a single girl here who won't have her fun."

"Get me in contact with one of them, and I can show you the signs."

"You've met Beate."

"Beate?"

"Freddie's friend. On the yacht."

"Oh. Her, too?"

"Yes."

"She appeared quite relaxed to me. Well, okay, yes, she seems like she's overcome her past experiences."

"I'm an amateur, but to me, it seems if someone really gets along fine, you don't have to tear open old wounds."

"Well . . ."

"It's okay. Word will spread why you're here, and if someone approaches you, then why not help them?"

Peter drank the last of his beer. "It would be an interesting professional challenge." Then he looked into my eyes. "Of course, there's an even bigger challenge here on the island."

I smiled at him.

"First Melbourne, then Manhattan, then an extraordinary incident during a test flight," he enumerated. "These events get talked about in expert circles, too. It's astonishing how relaxed you are and how you've handled it all."

"It's just pain, Peter. I don't strive for a repetition, but I don't have nightmares."

"Sure? Sometimes bad experiences come up years later."

"I'm not your patient, Peter. I don't need you."

"Many believe that until I start my treatment."

"I'm a Dragon, Peter."

"So what?"

"I'm different. How about this, I'll talk to you about my past. Would you like to start with my oldest memories?"

"Well, some problems result from childhood experiences."

"Would you be willing to go back five thousand years into the past?"

CHAPTER FORTY-SEVEN

Nanette came and took his empty glass of beer away. "Another?"

"I shouldn't," he replied and watched her exchange my empty glass for a full one. "You're drinking a lot."

"Don't draw wrong conclusions. Alcohol has no effect on me. It only contributes taste and nutrition."

"Oh." He placed one hand on top of the other. "Well, yes. Perhaps we should talk about my patient now. Sylvie. Where is she now?"

"I think she's training with the others."

"Training? Yes, that's fine. To rebuild muscles, right?"

"No. She didn't sustain any muscle weakness in space. Sylvie is part of our security team, like Beate."

"Security?" He smirked. "Beate didn't look like security personnel."

"They can be deceiving. The girls are able, even naked, to take on a Marines unit."

"Marines? You're pulling my leg."

"They've already proven it. There was an attempt to conquer the island and capture me. The attempt failed, and the soldiers were handed over to the Australian police. We didn't announce it publicly."

"It's hard to believe."

"Once you know their background, you'll understand. The girls were originally trained by the Cartel as killer commandos . . ."

Peter scooped up the remainder of milk foam from his cappuccino cup with a spoon. Then he set the cup down and placed his fingertips together.

"That was an exciting story. Now I understand what you've been talking about all along. It's astonishing that these women show no signs of psychosis. Unscientifically speaking, I'm assuming you have a stabilizing influence."

"Maybe. I give them respect, a home, and important jobs."

"You're giving them a role model *and* love." He smiled. "Don't deny it. You like them all very much. You're like a mother and a friend to them. A true *Protectress*. Even a passionate Protectress, right?"

"If the occasion arises, yes."

"I'm more and more curious about talking to your protégé."

"I believe you." I sensed my Companion approaching. "First there's someone else you should meet."

"Who is it?"

"My *Companion*."

CHAPTER FORTY-EIGHT

Tess remained standing at my side, and we watched Sylvie and Peter walk away.

"Good idea," Tess said. "Sylvie really wants to get over it, and having someone tell her how to manage it will help her."

"You think so?"

"I think her feelings of uncertainty are the worst for her. She has no noticeable problems she can work on fixing. She appears okay, even to herself, so she's distressed. She can't prove there's nothing wrong. Neither of us can." Tess shrugged. "If you consider where we came from, it's a miracle that we haven't gone nuts yet. Our, well, *conditioning* wasn't pleasant."

"You never mentioned it."

"No. That's the past. It was a different Tess, a Tess who didn't want anything more than to survive. I truly believed survival was the most important, and I've developed a very cynical attitude toward that. Okay, the men abused me, mutilated me, and drugged me. Then they taught me how to kill and showed me how I could control myself—how I had to control myself to survive. I know how to keep a completely cracked psycho on speed at bay."

"You're no psycho."

"Of course not. You took the drugs away that caused me trouble. You repaired the mutilations on my body. And, you've provided me with a new—better—purpose for my killer training and thus also repaired the mutilations in my head. I believe I'm healed, at least. Perhaps I wasn't even entirely injured yet."

"What do you mean by that?"

"My attitude toward the whole situation with the Cartel may have helped keep me stable. I always told myself, *Tess, that's not you.* Or *yes, you did this, but it's not your fault. It's for the drugs.* When you offered us a way out, the old Tess—the true Tess—gained control again."

She paused for a second. "Wait, that sounds wrong, I don't want to sound like I'm schizophrenic. I played a role in the past, and when you saved me, the stage play ended. I will never play that role again."

"Hum."

"I guess, it's the same with my girls. Those who didn't manage to develop such an attitude back then aren't around anymore. They were *sorted out.*"

She placed one hand on my shoulder. "Sylvie lived through the Cartel's torture. She can also get over her near-death experience. I'm positive about that."

"I feel a little bit bad about it."

Tess turned to me in surprise. "Why?"

"I don't just have selfless thoughts about it. We need Sylvie."

"What for?"

"Come with me."

The communication center was filled with people. It was almost time for dinner. No one was ever late to dinner except for extremely valid reasons. Otherwise, you would be on Nanette's shit list. It was the one rule on Velvet Island the inhabitants never dared to break.

I walked between the tables of students and teachers eagerly discussing the day's work or lessons to the pinboards. I picked up a card and pen. That alone sufficed to silence some of the conversations.

When I approached the board with the labeled card, it was so silent that you could hear me pin the card on the board.

The card contained two words, but it represented a mammoth project.

Wormhole generator.

PART SIX—EXPERIMENTS

CHAPTER FORTY-NINE

The light-blue ball on the screen before me slowly grew. The cameras outside captured more details on the cloud patterns.

Francine stood next to my pilot chair and handed me a cup of hot chocolate. "Nice."

"I'd like to see Neptune with my own eyes."

"So what? Do it."

I sipped at my chocolate. Then I looked up at her. "I don't want to waste air. I'd be doing just that if I go outside. The suit doesn't recycle."

"No. Of course. But when will we have this opportunity again?"

"Often. As long as the *Ryūjin* doesn't fly yet, the *Mischief* is our only space-worthy test carrier. We might return here on another test flight."

"Yes, sure. A pity you gave the others away."

Three years ago, I had ordered four steel bodies for our Barracudas, but we had only completed two when the invader came. The next two, *Menace* and *Mayhem,* would run on UN budget once they were ready.

"We simply can't afford to finish and operate two more, Francine. I decided to secure the two *Tigersharks* for us instead."

"For Tess' mission?"

"Exactly."

She sighed. "You can't have it all. I'd like to be with them, but I wouldn't miss this for anything in the world."

"I'd like to do their mission myself, but I can't be every-where. Mmm — perhaps I should've let Achrotzyber fly with you?"

Francine smiled joyously. "Oh yes. I think we'd get along well here. I'd really like to try him out."

"You haven't been together with him yet?"

"He's your Companion."

"So what?"

"Other than that, I don't know if I'd have fun with normal men afterward — after such a tool. Nah, I'd rather not risk it. I'll stick to getting pleasure at bars."

"You're more into quickies?"

"Oh, you'd be surprised how much time tough guys take once the pressure is gone and the first round is done."

"I'm not surprised."

"No? Well, you're a pro. I'm sure you know. Well, in any case, once I show them a little of what I've learned from you, they're wrapped around my finger or — should I say — my clit."

"Which is more fun."

"Certainly."

I raised my cup up to my lips. "Well, back to our test pro-gram. The kitchen stood the test well."

"The artificial gravity stood the test," Francine said. "I mean, sex in free fall is great, but I still prefer to drink my hot cocoa from a real cup."

"Me too."

These were just two topics to cover on our test program. First, we tested the creation of artificial gravity practically, that is, under acceleration of our Barracuda as well as in iner-tial flight.

The rationale behind it was simple. If it was possible to ac-celerate a Barracuda by kilometers per square second without turning the crew into pulp — because the accelerating nestle field affected its entire content — then why shouldn't it be possible to provide the interior with its own vector? It was possible, even if it meant a significantly higher control quark output.

Moreover, it had caused Armin and Gerard, our gravity field experts, some sleepless nights to protect this interior from destructive interferences and fluctuations. We had agreed on an emergency shutdown in case of the tiniest glitch. So far, there hadn't been any glitch.

Consequently, the second topic required us to observe and record the long-term effects of the control quark shower on the human body.

This was the main reason Francine and I were chosen for this test flight. Our odds of survival were much higher in case there were side-effects.

"How long do you think it will take for the *Youdjinn* to be mission-ready?" Francine asked.

"*Ryūjin,*" I automatically corrected. "*Lou-djinn.*"

Francine's Japanese was still strongly influenced by her French accent. She had to struggle with the mythical Dragon god's name.

"Yes, yes. So, how long?"

"So far, we've cataloged the parts that must fit inside the ship like fusion reactors, energy batteries, control quark emitters, air and water recycling, and so on. We also need room for operations and research, construction, living spaces, services, storage, and last but not least, hangars for Barracudas and Phoenix carriers."

Francine nodded, perhaps with a growing understanding for the complexity of ship-building.

"All these parts must be put together and wrapped in a hull of appropriate size. That's not rocket science for someone who can build aircraft carriers. But — "

I raised a finger. "The problem is that we don't know how

to build a wormhole generator yet. We don't know how large the generator will be. That will decide which of the rough sketches we will use to build the *Ryūjin*. Once we know the generator's size, we will lay the keel for the body of the spacecraft. From then on, I estimate that it will take up to three years until the *Ryūjin* can truly take off."

"Three years?"

"Three years isn't that long, considering the potential size of the largest generator and how big the ship will have to be to carry it. You'd have to consider the thousands of control quark emitters you must integrate into the ship's hull and the kilometers of wire you need to link them together. Then, of course, you have to make sure that everything functions properly if you really want to go into battle with that ship."

I winked at her. "It could go faster, but even if the Imperatrix personally shows up on the construction site, that won't cause miracles. My reputation isn't that threatening."

"So we'll fly around with this little one for the next three years?"

"No. The first Phoenix will be ready soon. Then we'll test how such a large chunk of metal can be handled. Meanwhile, we're working on the wormhole generator, so we'll know how big it must be."

"That always sounds so easy. It's like drilling a hole through a wall, right?"

"It's not that simple. We don't have a solid wall."

"Mmm. Then is it more like a tunnel in the sand?"

"Yes. Or, more like a tunnel underwater." I gazed at the wall behind Francine and pondered the problem. "We're actually creating a kind of vortex that sucks up everything around it. Why actually, if we only need the tunnel itself, not the sucking?"

"Do we really need a steady tunnel?"

"What?"

"Well, we only want to get one spaceship through. Then, we're going to let the tunnel collapse. So, why must the entire passage remain open if we only have to protect the ship from the *water* around it?"

"You're right. It doesn't have to . . . Excuse me. I must make a model of that."

I set my cup down and leaned over the dashboard.

"Jo?"

"Leave me."

"Jo, would you please switch the controls to me first? You surely don't want your great ideas to collide with Neptune."

"Oh."

CHAPTER FIFTY

"Aaawtriplejellycurseddamnedcrappyformulastuff!"
My angry hacking on the virtual keyboard didn't conjure up a better solution, sadly.

Francine didn't even try to calm me down. Instead, she asked, "Coffee or chocolate?"

"Coffee. Strong. Thanks."

She rose and walked to the back of the ship. Meanwhile, I jumped back to the start of my set of formulas.

"Okay. I have two singularities which I connect with each other in a way that they merge to form one singularity, but in that case, the distance between entry and exit is zero. Or I could have a tunnel with finite length between the two to determine a vector. But I'm limited to the speed of light again. That all doesn't add up."

I remembered a remark by Tim from my first term. The simplified formula sets we were using in some places were only applicable in a specific interval, to get around points of discontinuity. Was one of those formulas involved here?

Here.

Okay, if I replaced this formula with its complete counterpart, this derivative no longer matched and I had to re-work that resolution to c.

"Your coffee's getting cold, Jo."

Without looking at it, I took the cup and drank it in one gulp. "Thanks."

I didn't notice Francine taking the empty cup away.

If I merged this set of formulas now into the overall

package, I should get a true mathematical description of the wormhole. No, error. That didn't match yet. Ah yes, sure. If I replaced this formula, I had to take a different approach for the vectoring. When I finished entering the data into the computer, an isoline visualization of a wormhole appeared on the screen.

"Wow, Jo. You did it? Great!"

"Wait, Francine. I described a static wormhole here, meaning, the complete tunnel. I'm not even sure whether it all fits."

"Why? What else can that be?"

"This isn't really a wormhole, more precisely put, it's the mathematical model of a wormhole. The first question we have to consider is whether this model correctly matches reality. It's already darn hard to survey a wormhole if you have one, if you don't have any, it's even harder."

Francine grinned. "Yes, okay. I understand that. So, you've got a model that matches your assumptions here. And you surely have some clues as to whether it closely matches reality or not. Don't you?"

"Yes, sure. It's based on formulas that passed the reality check in other cases, after all. Otherwise, I could have just painted the graphics."

"Good. Where's the problem then?"

"That there isn't merely one solution, from my point of view. If colleagues on Earth developed a working formula set, too, it wouldn't have to be the same as this one, and you can't simply make the assumptions, limitations, and simplifications of different formula sets match. That's the frustrating thing we've been grappling with for the last year. There are so many possible approaches and no way to pinpoint which one is the most accurate. Your idea with the water tunnel made me think of a different approach. Based on that model, it seems to work."

"Really? But I don't know anything about wormholes."

"Then I must tell you how I invented the Meier effect."

CHAPTER FIFTY-ONE

"Copulating quarks," Francine repeated while shaking her head. "Okay, that's just a picture, but it seems to help. You've solved a problem within a few days, which all your experts have been racking their brains over for the past year. Don't you call that *genius?*"

"It was a chance hit."

"It was not. Okay. Our discussion evolved by chance. Then you sat down and didn't let go until you had a solution."

I slid down in my chair and placed my toes on the screen's edge. "Well, okay."

I contemplated Francine's words for a bit. "Anyone down there could have done the same."

"All of them had the same information, right?"

"More or less. At the University, we have a few more wormhole readings. I should check them against my model."

"They should be on the computer, too. We have the same instruments aboard and the same programs Eduardo wrote for Martha. His comparison programs can't do anything without patterns."

For a moment, I was stunned—but Francine *was* clever. Other than the two students she'd just mentioned, she hadn't gone to the University and had no ambitions to enroll. I wouldn't have put that past her.

"Of course. I didn't check the operative data, but only the scientific files and the package wasn't included there."

"Even a genius can overlook things."

"I'm not a genius."

"What are you then?"

Yes, what was the reason I could achieve this break-through? Was I so much smarter than all the others? No. My results during my studies were comparable to my tenure. I wasn't smarter than Reginald or Pam, only more unconventional in my thinking.

At least, that had been true during my studies. With the aid of my nano-enhanced brain — the *Analogy* — I could memorize data, facts, and formulas much better. I could also juggle more ideas simultaneously and more complex problems in a short amount of time. I could compare patterns and connect open threads, without losing critical points. That had doubtlessly helped me dig through the heap of formulas and combine them the right way.

The answer was easy. "I'm Dragon."

"Okay," she simply said. "Do you want to cross-check your solution first or write your research report right away and transmit it to Earth? We're behind the sun right now, so we have to fly a bit farther."

"I must validate the results first. Then I must consider how I want to publish them."

"Why?"

"The last thing I need is people talking about the *Meier hole.*"

"So?" Francine contemplatively stared at my toes. "Then let's stop talking about it and start working it."

Chapter Fifty-Two

Okay, I had the model for a tunnel with a gravitational funnel opening to free space at each end. In other words, it was a rotating ring-like singularity within which the space-time upended inward. The connecting upends created the tunnel that allowed a spaceship to bridge interstellar distances within survivable timeframes. Inside the tunnel, the laws of nature in space still applied—more specifically, the laws of nature in the immediate neighborhood of a singularity. The location of an object inside the tunnel could only be described in relation to the two involved singularities.

Sadly, the entire model didn't match our readings at all. Those were much more complex than the ones my model could theoretically create. What was the reason? Well, my model postulated a static tunnel—one moment it's there, the next, it isn't. That didn't match our observations on the evolution of wormholes at all.

So I needed parameters I could vary over time. I'd have to introduce them step by step. What happened if I reduced the ring's circumference to zero? Did that necessarily have to have an effect on the tunnel's circumference?

The answer to my current equation system was simple—yes. If I wasn't satisfied with that—and I wasn't satisfied—I had to improve the model, so that it allowed rings of different sizes at both ends on the first step.

Okay.

Francine came and left, bringing food and drinks to me. Sometimes she would put it into my hands. I ate mechanically, not focusing on the taste of the food or drinks. When I finished my meal, Francine cleaned up after me.

On a number of virtual screens all around me, the formulas grew to grotesque fractal structures. Meanwhile, the animated model of the wormhole tunnel — the only graphical display I granted us — became more detailed and vibrant. *Mischief's* computer complained about the increasing load.

My updated model could bear a unilaterally created ring singularity that wrapped into itself and toward a destination point like a thread. Then it expanded the destination point to a ring and at the same time expanded the thread to a tunnel. Next, the ring singularity at the departure point collapsed to a point, followed by the tunnel. Without the supporting tunnel structure, the gravitational funnel around the starting point faded away.

"Great," Francine commented. "That's a wormhole's life cycle?"

"No. The model is good, but it doesn't match the readings. For all I know, our readings require you to start with two points that eventually meet each other, then expand in length and diameter turning into a tunnel. After use, the tunnel collapses."

"Oh. So you must change the model?"

"I don't know. The big problem with the other model is that the destination point inevitably moves into a gravitation funnel's center when you create the wormhole."

"And that means?"

"That you arrive right inside the sun and thoroughly mess up its energy balance. Very unpleasant."

"So that model's wrong, too?"

"No, it's incomplete. It lacks the one component it needs to create a second gravitation tunnel close to another without the two slipping into each other."

"Is that a question of power?"

I considered that. "Good! Yes, energy feed is one answer. Only, where in this model does the energy have to go into?"

My gaze fell on the slowly pulsating model. If I colored it flesh-red, it would temporarily resemble a vagina. This was my area of expertise.

Okay, the idea of a complete penetration put a lot of stress on the imaginary model. I wondered how the model had to be composed so that the tunnel contour could be adapted to the shape of the inserted body.

CHAPTER FIFTY-THREE

Francine came with two cups of hot chocolate.

"Thanks," I acknowledged her off while saving another intermediate formula set.

What would the model look like if the first ring didn't have to remain open — that is, if I wanted to insert a love ball? That only required a minor change in my formula set.

"Hey!" Francine leaned over the model image. "Great! That looks slippery!"

"Slippery? Yes. You could put it that way." I couldn't help but grin while I took my cup out of her hand.

"I particularly like that there's no complete tunnel at any point in time. The space-time warping remains limited to the minimum you need for a solid body's transport."

"The funnel appears to be smaller, too."

"Right. The gravitational forces affecting the start and destination points are significantly lower."

"Does that have any effect on energy consumption?"

"Theoretically, yes. If the warp affects a smaller area in space, that inevitably requires less energy."

"Do you have any clue how much energy we will save?"

"No. I don't even know how to create such a structure. Roughly speaking, it must be similar to a cake knife. You basically reach out with a grav field and warp space. But what such a field should consist of — no idea."

Francine stepped over to her own dashboards. "Actually, I wanted to tell you that we can send a report in about an hour. But you didn't get to writing the report, did you?"

"No. What I have are step-by-step changes to the formulas. I think that's mandatory for understanding the final product. If you tried to take the formulas apart now, you wouldn't know where to start."

"Oh, don't worry. I surely don't want to do that."

"Good. So I have an hour left to write a short text for it? That should be enough time to write a summary at least. I'll have plenty of time before the first question from Earth can return. How long will it take?"

"Three to four hours each way," Francine said without consulting her board.

"That will do. Well, I should write the summary in a way that they can start without asking me questions. We can hardly discuss anything that way."

"That would take Dragon patience." Francine winked at me.

"Yees . . ." I thought of my Companion, whom I had left behind on Earth. He wanted to come along but had advised against it himself. It wasn't advisable for both of us to take the same risk, and of the two of us, I was better qualified, scientifically speaking.

Companion?

"Achrotzyber?!" I'd almost spilled my chocolate.

Francine looked at me.

Did you want to talk with me?

Yes. Wait, please. I had to tell Francine first. "I'm in contact with Achrotzyber. And there's *no delay!*"

"Phew."

Mighty, we're communicating across a distance of about four light hours, and there's no delay. That means that our communication isn't limited by the speed of light.

Of course not. After all, it is not light.

You knew that?

Francine watched my astonished face.

Companion, I apologize. I tried to apply the human concept of

164

humor. I failed.

Instead, you succeeded in pulling my leg.

That is impossible. Oh, I understand. Yes, I got you, true?

You did.

So what can I do for you, Companion?

You can tell Armin that I've developed a general formula set which describes the graviton structure of wormholes. I will send my report of the formula set to Earth in about an hour.

Armin is here. Shall I tell him now?

Go ahead. But make sure he's sitting down.

I gazed at Francine. "He's telling Armin."

"Oh, poor boy!"

"He'll get over it." After all, he was our professor for gravitational fields, so he was supposed to deal with my results.

Companion. Armin wants to know whether you solved the problem of the attraction of local gravitation sinks — whether you know where additional energy must be applied.

No, I didn't. I've found a different approach where this problem is avoided. My solution doesn't describe the Jelly wormholes, but a significantly more flexible and more economical approach. Francine describes the model as slippery.

Slippery?

Armin should watch the step-by-step formula refinement in the animated graphic display first, and the formula derivation afterward. I recorded the intermediate steps.

I will tell him. Once we have the data, may I address their questions to you?

He should read through all the data first and perhaps take a nap over it. I've got a few nights to catch up on.

I will tell him that. Good rest.

I'll rest once the data is on the way. Bye.

With a sigh, I conjured another virtual window up and began to type up my summary report.

CHAPTER FIFTY-FOUR

I never had trouble waking up in my entire life. I woke up, and I was ready. That was useful for a whore with irregular break times, for a full-time student with two side jobs, and for a thief hunted by Cartel killers. For a Dragoness, it was a matter of course, I thought.

I was puzzled when I needed several minutes to wake up fully, and that I had to get upright rather cautiously after.

Is that a warning sign for radiation damage?
— That's a sign for a long catch-up phase. —
How long?
— Twenty-six hours. —
Uh-oh.

I forced myself to get up quickly and dared the few steps into the shower cabin, where I granted myself a brief, cold refreshment. After, I ticked the entry for radiation damage in the test log off — *below limit of detection.*

Even if I didn't need to wash away dirt or sweat — thanks to my nanos — I enjoyed the occasional shower. The latter wasn't on our test list, though.

After showering, I went to the pantry. According to the log, Francine ate her last meal eleven hours ago. So it was time to surprise her with a tasty breakfast.

For ingredients, I found vegetable paste and dough paste in different flavors, rice and potato mash powder, sauce paste, cheese paste, fruit and chocolate paste, freeze-dried ice cream powder. We had anything on board that could be turned into paste or powder and didn't cause flatulence or downdrafts.

We made our meals by adding recycled water to the pastes and powders. Hardy's food synthesizer and microwave oven — we called our clever student's invention a nanowave — performed miracles with these ingredients. We could choose from potato and vegetable cakes, cheese wraps, noodle variations or fresh bread rolls. Beyond that, the computer made sure we wouldn't suffer vitamin deficiency, especially calcium and vitamin D.

Compared to Nanette's homemade food or Nico's Greek specialties, our food onboard was spartan. In my opinion, we deserved something better after my breakthrough and after about half of the test program. My synthesis nanos would have to help me, and I'd have to *persuade* Hardy's magic box a bit.

Francine squealed with delight when I held the plate under her nose. She instantly sat up in her pilot chair and pulled the little table out from under the dashboard.

"Carpaccio of vegetable coins with apple-Balsamico-hazelnut vinaigrette, here you go."

"Where did you get that from?"

"From the kitchen. I had to do a little magic."

"Yes, indeed. Oh, that smells good."

"*Bon appétit.*"

"*De même.*"

My pilot enjoyed every bite, and I did, too. The dishes were empty much too soon, and Francine looked a bit disappointed.

"That was just for starters."

"What? You made more?"

"Sure. Wait."

I took her plate and went back to the pantry. The nanowave was finished. I just had to decorate the second dish and order the third. When it was ready, I presented the second course.

"Here. Please, enjoy. Truffles paté with cranberry sauce."

Francine ogled the crunchy bread crust. "I wasn't aware we could cook this kind of food with our kitchen appliance."

"Me neither, until I tried it," I admitted. "I'll send Hardy a few proposals for improvement. Don't let it get cold."

I didn't have to say that twice. Soon our plates were empty again, and I fetched the next course. This time, I served the food in a glass.

"What's that?" Francine asked.

"Champagne sorbet with lime brittle."

She tried it. "Wow. I'd let myself get laid for that anytime."

"That can be arranged."

"Later." She tried another spoonful and rolled her eyes. "Great. I dare say your food beats Nanette's kitchen by light hours. How did you make all this delectable food?"

"With nano technology."

"Okay. But where do the recipes come from?"

"Mmm — I make them up."

"The world has lost a cook in you. Thank you!"

"We're not finished yet."

"I had hoped for that."

During my preparations, I mused about the main course. The magic had its limits. Nevertheless, Francine beamed when I brought her the next plate. "Herbs-and-cheese-filled Tortellini with tomato confit."

"That was so good," Francine raved. "Just great."

"Thanks. Would you like a dessert?"

"You've got more? Bring it on!"

Grinning, I disappeared to the pantry to fetch my last surprise.

"Diced fruit timbale in jelly on chocolate sauce with nut-rose-pralines Arabian style. Enjoy."

"Jo, you outdid yourself."

"Thanks. I had the appetite for something else."

Francine sampled a bite, swallowed, and licked her lips. "Mmm . . . I could get used to this."

I sat down and began to enjoy my creation.

"Did you frequently cook before?"

"Only once, in Palermo," I admitted. "I always like to eat something good, so I tried my hand at cooking. When you lived off raw fish or rat for a while, you learn to value good food. Our regular food onboard isn't bad compared to raw fish or rat."

"But if you aren't experienced in cooking, how did you manage to create all of this?"

"I didn't say I had no experience. I've only done it once before. I guess it's like sex in a way. If you know how others can please you and how good you can feel when it's done right, then it's not hard to please others. Add a little imagination, and you've got the recipes. Of course, you must copy or derive the preparation."

"Derive?"

"Well. You should consider in advance how the chemical and physical processes must run so that the result looks right."

"Oh, Jo!"

CHAPTER FIFTY-FIVE

A rmin remained silent for a suspiciously long time. But then again, I'd sent him the comprehensive version of my approach only five days ago. He was probably still trying to digest the formula set I had created in those two sleepless days. Still, I expected the first questions to come through long ago.

Francine was already sleeping. According to our onboard clock, it was early in the evening on the island, the time when researchers assembled around Nanette. I called my Companion.

Mighty.

Yes, Companion. I did not want to disturb you. Did you get enough rest?

Quite. How's Armin doing?

He is in good health. Your report excited him very much, and he slept little in the last days, but he is enthusiastic. He froze the regular lectures in favor of the project.

Which project?

Yours. The wormhole generator. He said the way you designed the formulas, they are almost a programming blueprint for control quarks. The students are turning that blueprint into code right now. Armin, Tim, and Gerard are designing stronger projectors. Armin wants to finish a prototype as soon as possible.

What does he need that for so soon? It will take years to build a spaceship for it.

No. He said he estimates the energy consumption for a Meier gravtunnel is so low that the necessary reactors and batteries can easily fit into a Phoenix carrier.

So small?

You had insinuated in your report that the energy requirements are significantly lower if one travels in a bubble instead of maintaining an entire tunnel. Should the simulations confirm this, only a Phoenix would have to be refitted.

Great! Tell Armin once he's got something for me, he should send me a package with the simulation and programming. Then I'll have something to do out here.

Naturally.

Oh. Please tell Rashid that we'll ask him for a Phoenix soon. He'd probably like to have some time to pull political strings.

Yes. That is an approach I do not understand yet.

It's difficult indeed. He must move his conversation partners to an extrapolation that lets his wishes appear favorable to all involved. However, as he doesn't know their current extrapolations — and humans often don't understand their motivations, as irrational as they sometimes are — he needs time for that. Once the extrapolations match, it's easy for him to act fast.

Ah. Like it is easier to develop the programming for a Meier gravtunnel once the theoretical model is completely described.

Like that, yes.

Meier gravtunnel? Who had come up with this label? Okay, I shouldn't complain. It sounded much better than *Meier hole.*

The prospect of starting a prototype within a few weeks or months appealed to me. Of course, the most important finding was that we didn't have to build a humongous death star just to hold the generator. The first cost estimate for such a project had startled even Rashid. The workforce to build it was so great that I couldn't even figure out the number of skilled workers we would need to hire.

Even more stressful was the thought of how many hidden errors could slip through undetected during construction. That haunted me. The last thing I needed was a sudden interference during the wormhole transit because someone had soldered a cable in the wrong place. With a Phoenix, I saw significantly better odds.

CHAPTER FIFTY-SIX

"Anything new?" Francine asked cheerfully, dropping into her pilot seat. "Is the tunnel generator done already?"

"Yes. Armin is sending the data."

She jerked around and stared at me. "Really? I was just joking."

"Yesterday, you would've been joking. Okay, the real generator isn't built yet, but the programming for it is ready to be tested. We have the program code that derives a vector for the start and destination coordinates then directs the grav field projectors to create a bubble."

"A bubble?"

"The piece of tunnel that's needed to travel between the two coordinates."

"Ah, okay. The energy saver version."

"Exactly."

"And what will you do with the code?"

"Cross-check it. I asked Armin to send me the data so that I can utilize my time aboard."

"Hum. I thought you're already utilizing your time aboard. After all, we're on a research mission."

"Well, yes, along with that."

"Instead of sleep." She threatened me with raised index finger. "Don't go too far. It's our island people's turn to work." She mused. "Or do you want to test the results right away?"

"How would I test the results?"

"Well, I thought if you only have to trigger the grav field projectors differently, the *Mischief* might be able to do it, too?"

"Create a wormhole with our projectors? No."

"No, a bubble just for us. Just an idea."

"Oh." I thought about the possibility of such a feat. Why not? The projectors were powerful enough to erect a nestle field and a shield together. After that, they still had the power to create a cake knife, even though the amount of energy to project one was gigantic. How did the energy budget of a cake knife over a distance of several light seconds look against that of a Meier tunnel bubble of less than a hundred meters?

Francine watched me with fascination as I produced several new projections, juggled with the formulas, adjusted parameters and conjured up graphic displays.

"Okay," I finally said.

"Okay?"

"I still lack the control software, so I did a conservative rough estimate. Yes, one of our reactors suffices to create a tunnel bubble. We could create such a field. We'd only have to accelerate the *Mischief* to at least a quarter light speed without killing ourselves."

"And gain distance from the sun?"

"What? Oh, no, that applied to the other formula. Roughly estimated, a few light seconds distance to the next planet should do."

"Very well. We could extend our flight schedule."

I watched her for a moment. She didn't seem to worry about anything going wrong. Just the opposite, she seemed to be looking forward to it.

"Yes, we could."

"Fine. What can I do to prepare?"

"We need a *Mischief* in optimal shape. Flawlessly trimmed."

"Okay. I'll review the logs and start a deep analysis."

"Do that. And I'll get us cover." We should be well-prepared for such a test flight. *Mighty, I've got something more.*

I guessed that. What?

Could you ask Sylvie to expand her next training flight farther out?

How much farther?

Let's say, a few light minutes beyond Mars' orbit. We could be there in two weeks time.

I will propose a tandem flight to her. I will take the second Barracuda. Our students shall practice rendezvous maneuvers between Menace *and* Mayhem. *Maybe we also simulate the rescue from a surprisingly arising distress situation.*

That's about how I envisaged it. I wouldn't call UN pilot candidates *students,* but that was up to him. He was the teacher, so they were his students.

And what exactly is your plan, Companion?

I'm going to reprogram the Mischief *and create a Meier tunnel bubble. According to my rough calculation, we have enough power for the process. Of course, I can only safely tell that once I've received Armin's data.*

I should destroy our radio station first.

CHAPTER FIFTY-SEVEN

A chrotzyber hadn't destroyed the radio station. Two days later, Armin's data arrived. Two days after that the programming was integrated into my model and tested. It took me three days of careful work to integrate the programming blueprints into *Mischief's* controls and to repeat Francine's deep analysis.

She watched me compare the results.

"Everything seems to match," I found out.

"Fine. What are we waiting for?"

"For Sylvie and Achrotzyber. I want to have backup nearby before starting the experiment."

"I understand. You had a bad experience before. It can't hurt to be careful, right?"

"Exactly."

"Well, a few days more won't matter now. Anything else?"

"I know now that *Mischief* can brave the transit. I want to be prepared to face incidentals, like stray radiation and such."

"Oh. Okay."

Francine seemed to be unperturbed and entirely free of worries. Was that normal? I remembered what Tess told me about herself and indirectly about her girls. They'd had to adapt in an extreme way, since whoever didn't comply died.

Then I came along and freed them from the biochemical rape and the permanent threat of physical abuse. I gave their life new meaning. I was kind to them, respected them, cared for them. In return, I earned a form of devotion from them that went beyond death, as Jasmine had demonstrated.

I assumed that Francine wouldn't object to my plans even if she had concerns. Perhaps she wouldn't even admit her fear to herself, because the idea that I would recklessly put her in danger was unthinkable to her. She wouldn't stand back if there were any residual risks I was ready to bear.

She wouldn't hold me back. She'd stand by me through anything. So I had to take a different approach.

"Francine?"

"Yes?"

"What could I have forgotten? What didn't I check? I fear I can't see the forest for all the trees. I can only think of formulas."

"Oh. Okay, I'll think about it. Coffee?"

"A hot chocolate, gladly, thanks."

She disappeared into the pantry.

What had I failed to see?

CHAPTER FIFTY-EIGHT

Francine returned and handed me a cup of hot chocolate. "I just had a spontaneous idea," she said.

"What?"

"I thought of your test flight with the Taipan."

"You mean the interferences that disintegrated the bird? No, I can rule that out."

"No. I thought of the control problem. You grab the stick and get an unexpectedly strong reaction. For example, how fast are we accelerating when we enter the bubble?"

"Okay, I can compute that. Our artificial gravity field should neutralize that."

"Can the controller change the field so quickly?"

"In principle, I checked that, so yes. Those are not entirely independent processes. The controller receives the signals together with the nestle field, or like here, with the field for the bubble. That's only a special kind of nestle field."

"If you say so. But if I understand correctly, there are additional outside forces to consider."

"Exactly. Yes, I accounted for them."

No, Jo, I corrected myself. *You've accounted for those outside forces that your model predicts. You have no clue which possible overshoots your model doesn't take into consideration. After all, our formulas only provide us with a good approximation of reality. The approximation is good enough to make our technical marvels work, but what if we pass a discontinuity point upon transit into the bubble that's not accounted for in the formula?*

The idea was haunting. But what choices did we have to

find out more? We couldn't ask anyone how a wormhole transit worked.

Yes, we could.

Zoe had met someone not born on Earth. Zoe knew a *Caretaker,* and they had talked about the wormhole passage. My *recollection* contained her statement.

— Any higher life forms' brain activity will be stopped during the passage. Brain death. —

Oops.

CHAPTER FIFTY-NINE

— For carriers of the essence then there's a cold start with the stored memories. —

I already knew that, even without my *Analogy* reminding me. I had experienced a cold start already. Only my death, years ago in Hawaii, hadn't been as unpleasant as Eva had told Zoe.

— It's a slow, painful, cruel, agonizing death, because you consciously experience your mind fading away. —

If all this applied, there were only two people in our entire system who could survive such a journey — me and Achrotzyber. Francine would have no chance.

If we followed through with this test flight, I'd probably find her lifeless body next to me, with her face disfigured by inexplicable agony, after I completely rebooted. That was out of the question.

On the other hand, we couldn't give up now. Which effects of the wormhole transit caused brain death?

— No data. —

Okay. So I had to significantly refine my model again to reflect the effects of the transit inside a spaceship — and not just with regard to gravitational fields, but also in relation to radiation, magnetism, and electrical fields, including electromagnetic induction. Was that enough?

I pushed the idea aside. Yes, this modeling was necessary. But first, I had to prove the effect could occur in a classical wormhole transit.

To prove that, I had to switch to the other model. Okay, I

didn't know how to twist the exit away from a star. I didn't have to know. For my purpose, it sufficed to make a model of a wormhole in empty space and verify the problem within that model.

No, I didn't have to do all that on my own. The classical model already existed at the University, and we had long ago created models for cosmic radiation, magnetic fields, and electrical potentials as preparation for our current mission.

I could request the classical model data from the University. Until that arrived, I could integrate the other effects into my model of the Meier tunnel. I'd only have to re-run this integration with the other model once it arrived.

For a moment, I mused that it might be cocky if I believed I could find a solution to a problem that even the Jelly spaceship constructors couldn't solve. But then again, I didn't know if the constructors of the Jelly ships had been in a hurry or not to start their campaign. After all, Zoe and her followers departed without solving this problem either.

Moreover, the constructors and users of the Jelly motherships didn't know about the Meier effect. They'd had hundreds of thousands of years for this advancement to arise but never came up with it.

So if I was allowed to invent the Meier effect, why shouldn't I consider other improvements, too?

I could still hope that the Meier gravtunnel with its significantly softer transitions might have less drastic side effects. To prove these hopes true was the major purpose of my efforts.

CHAPTER SIXTY

Francine snuck in and quietly sat down in her seat. Her enthusiasm had noticeably disappeared.

"It's not because of you, Francine. In my *memory,* I found a hint from Zoe I must follow up."

"Dangerous?"

"The transit is unconditionally lethal."

Francine let her breath escape between her teeth with a hiss. "But then, the Lionheart —"

"Died upon leaving our solar system, yes. With every other intelligent life aboard the ship. They all knew the outcome, and they still left. You know why?"

"Why?"

"They knew they'd be resurrected, with all their *memories.*"

"But how?"

"Similar to the way I took over Zoe's memories. It's a special Dragon ability. It's the same ability that allowed me to overcome death in Hawaii."

"Your feigned death."

"My *death,* Francine."

She remained silent for a while.

"I don't suppose you could teach me that within a few days, could you?"

"No, and that wouldn't be a real solution. I want to find out what killed them so I can prevent it from happening."

"How are you going to do that?"

"Francine, I didn't study Dragon technology for years to surrender to such a trifle."

"Of course not." She smiled again. "I don't quite understand why some people fear the Dragon in you. The most dangerous thing about you is your mind."

"In this regard, I'm in good company. And now I must dig
through this formula set."

"Naturally. Hot chocolate?"

"Hot chocolate."

CHAPTER SIXTY-ONE

Francine's praise went down like hot chocolate, but it didn't help me. I had one day left until our rendezvous with *Menace* and *Mayhem,* but I had no solution yet. My model seemed complete, but it didn't show me a reason for the gradual termination of higher life-forms' brain activities.

The entire situation could be reduced to one single problem. There was just too little data. Without empirical tests, there was no way to find out whether my model resembled reality, or whether the trick that cheated light speed had unknown side effects.

Perhaps electrical fields couldn't travel faster than light? Nonsense. Of course, they could. The Jelly mothership computers were still there, too, and they were running on electricity. Or did the computers hibernate, too? This thought was truly terrifying, because that meant no one was available to control the gravtunnel during the tunneling phase.

Then the envelope fields of fusion reactors would fail, too. The electrical charges of starter batteries would eventually fade away resulting in the spaceship arriving at its destination electrically dead. Even more puzzling was the fact that the Jellies depended on bioelectricity to survive. If the electrical charges gradually faded during the trip, how did the Jellies survive the transit? No, this wasn't the problem.

I sat straight up, and Francine watched me with curiosity.

"Okay. Here's the plan. Since the model won't tell me, we can't do the faster-than-light flight together."

"So it's canceled?"

"Wait. We'll exercise a distress situation so that the pilot students on *Menace* and *Mayhem* have something to do. You're going to evacuate during this exercise."

"Only me. Okay."

"I'll stay aboard. After you evacuate, we'll break up. Once I've gained enough distance from *Mayhem* and *Menace*, let's say a few light seconds, I can do a very short tunnel flight alone. The tunnel flight can only end in two ways."

Francine wouldn't like the first. I smiled at her.

"The first possibility is that the lethal effect takes place, and I'll need a reboot. The measurement instruments onboard should have picked up something along with their readings of long-term radiation. Once we've analyzed the data, I can refine my model accordingly."

She seemed to be taking it well, so I continued.

"The second possibility is that there is no effect at all. We still get readings for my model, but we also prove that this kind of faster-than-light travel isn't lethal. Whatever the outcome, we'll win."

Francine was about to argue. I spoke up before she said a word.

"In any case, you'll follow me and pick me up. Whatever happens, my *Companion* will find me."

My pilot didn't appear to be happy about my plan.

"Francine, I know, to you it sounds as if I want to get rid of you. That's the way it is. I must ask you to leave because I can't teach you how to be reborn."

"I don't like that you'll be far away in case you need help. What will you do if your flight doesn't end after a short distance? You'll be stranded somewhere in space all alone with provisions for only a few weeks."

"I can shut down my metabolism so that I don't need anything. I'm sure the flight will go as planned. The only thing uncertain is the flight's effects on me."

CHAPTER SIXTY-TWO

Without Francine's familiar presence, I felt lonely. It was dead silent around me. To avoid interference with the readings, I had switched all unnecessary aggregates off.

"*Mischief,* this is *Menace* calling."

"Yes, Sylvie, what is it?"

Pause. I counted in my mind—*eight, nine, ten.*

"Do you want to re-think this plan?"

"No. I must conduct this test flight before letting a single non-Dragon go through a transit."

Okay, we could have done two test transits—one without me, and afterward, one with me. But that would have cost us time, and I wasn't ready to give precious time away.

I had already strapped myself to my seat, put my arms and legs through the loops that should prevent sudden movements. I also disabled my power boost, so that I couldn't accidentally tear the loops off.

The artificial gravity remained active for two reasons. First, with the gravity turned on, no potential emitted fluids could fly around freely and enter my air passages. My stomach, bowels, and bladder were empty anyway. I even interrupted the production of new digestive liquids. Second, it diverted the outside forces pulling at my ship. The effectivity of leaving it active was yet to be tested.

"In that case, good luck from us all."

"Thanks."

The entire transit was computer-controlled. Achrotzyber had correctly pointed out that I didn't necessarily have to be on board as a pilot. I agreed with him.

Since I didn't have to drive the ship, I acted as an additional measurement tool — an indispensable one.

The radio was an unnecessary device — at least immediately before transit. So it shut down as planned, just like the screens before me and the lighting.

Silence remained, except for the sound of my breathing and heartbeat. The darkness was absolute. I could feel the belts' even pressure and smell the slightly stuffy, metallic recycled air. I was going through classic sensory deprivation. It was like torture, but I didn't panic. I had experienced worse before. Instead, I imagined the taste of chocolate.

The *Mischief* was accelerating away from the sun, reaching high numbers. She had been doing that the whole day, like her sister-ships — which were following at an increasingly safe distance.

I wanted to have a clear margin above the postulated threshold of a quarter light speed, and I also wanted to keep a safe distance of at least a half light day from the Sun.

Once it reached forty percent *c,* the *Mischief* would change her inner nestle field from drive to a neutral protective cover. The ship would reconfigure her outer protective field to a tunnel bubble, which would expose the close vicinity to gravitational forces of a nascent black hole. Then the *Mischief* would toss itself and its contents through the ring singularity into her own miniverse. From there, she should emerge on schedule sixty seconds later and a modest three light days away through a second ring singularity.

This transit would take place only a few more breaths ahead.

Three.

Two.

One.

Now!

Dizziness.
Up is down.
Inside is outside.
I see a humming, feel blue, hear coldness.

CHAPTER SIXTY-THREE

How long was I out? Am I awake? I didn't hear or see anything, but I felt the belts holding me. There was a metallic taste in my mouth, as well. Did I bite my tongue?

Heal.

— Confirmed. —

Ah, my *Analogy* was still there. *Status?*

— Bite wound on the tongue. Healing process initiated. Slight nausea suppressed. Sense of balance off. No further impairments. —

I didn't die?

— No. A restart wasn't necessary. —

The screens woke up as well. At the same time, I felt a slight plucking in my head. I focused on it.

Companion?

Hello, Mighty. I'm okay. All went as planned. All clear.

I feel your thoughts from over a significant distance.

I've never been that far away before. So there's a limit to our communication at three or more light days. We must observe that more closely, but not now. Let me check the instruments first.

We will stay on our interception course.

According to the plan, Mischief *should be decelerating already. Yes, according to the dashboard, she is decelerating. But I'm getting a sequence of ambers now. Let me examine that.*

The symbol for the batteries briefly turned red. One of the fusion reactors increased its output to bear the additional power consumption. When the reactors began to recharge the batteries, the battery symbol changed back to amber.

The outer shield was stressed by the interstellar dust it had to push away. The nestle field worked hard to slow us down. Both shields needed enough power to drain the batteries.

The diagram that read my position relative to the Sun showed — to my surprise — nothing. What was going on? I carefully pulled my hands out of the loops. As soon as I was free, I sifted through some diagrams.

The transit consumed slightly more power than I had anticipated. That was why the batteries were nearly empty. Maybe it was caused by weakness in the bubble field? No, its efficiency factor was better by two orders of magnitude.

Let me see what I can do. With a little fine tuning and a few precautions against rounding differences in the coarse programming, two more orders of magnitude should be achievable. I probably couldn't ask for more from a small Barracuda.

Creating the first ring singularity had consumed the largest amount of energy, with a smaller peak to stabilize the entry point. Once the first ring was created, it took less power to maintain the bubble. I had to work on my model again. The space-time structure seemed to resist change in a way my model didn't incorporate yet — because I had only just found out about it. This kind of inertia had also affected the artificial gravity field. The log showed clear peaks at the moment of transit, followed by post-pulse oscillations that weren't completely compensated for by the ship. The *Mischief* couldn't be blamed for that, since she was programmed that way. For the moment of transit, we had to give the programming more leeway — and perhaps even a specific routine for just these peaks' compensation.

I browsed through the other instruments' readings. There was nothing peculiar with the temperature throughout the transit. Radiation? The log showed slightly increased ionization. There had been minor variations in the magnetic field, and a kind of intermittent electromagnetic pulse, which the computer was shielded against. Nevertheless, the inner nestle shield seemingly filtered the effect. At least its correction mechanisms showed the same oscillation patterns as the pulse.

If this pulse was an indication of the killer effect—just a bit stronger and *whoosh,* all brain waves would have been blown away—then the new transit method protected me. Jelly motherships entered the wormhole entirely without nestle field and artificial gravitation, which had to be way more unpleasant.

Ideas on how to integrate these effects into the model formed in the back of my mind.

Not now, I called myself to order.

I had to check for other critical readings. The symbol for the repair nanos glowed amber, and the one next to it indicated its value had been critical before. Why? The log showed signs of wear at the control quark emitters. That was not good, but it could have been connected to the lack of fine adjustment. I'd take care of that.

Amber for navigation—so there was a deviation, that had to be expected due to the coarse programming. The instruments showed a covered distance of—*three light years?*

CHAPTER SIXTY-FOUR

I refined the model and let the simulation run again. Then I repeated the process to make sure I hadn't missed anything. No, it remained the same. The calculation yielded a tunnel distance of about three point one eight light years.

I took a deep breath.

Mighty.

Companion, it seems as if I'm not getting closer to you. We are flying at a third light speed, and I do not notice a difference. Shall I accelerate the flotilla?

Negative. You should decelerate. I'm whole and will program the Mischief *to turn back. I'll return once I've reversed the speed vector and the batteries are recharged.*

We could meet earlier if we continued to follow you.

That's irrelevant, Mighty. Our model had a little glitch. The tunnel field proved to be more efficient than I expected. As a result, I went three light years.

That is catastrophic.

No. That's a true breakthrough in interstellar travel. Moreover, I didn't die, so this kind of space travel is significantly more pleasant than a Jelly wormhole. As Francine put it – slippery.

I don't understand slippery, Companion.

I must cross-check the programming now. I want to be sure that I find my way back and won't overshoot.

While I was at it, I might as well do the fine adjustments and the shielding for the transition. That might allow me to remain clear during transit and actively follow the flight.

I mentally noted that after my return I'd take the highest

tenure and walk through the code with them to clean it up. The current programming was completed with all due diligence but was in large parts a hastily patched-up cobble work. If used on a Phoenix, the current programming would end in a disaster. Regardless, the cobble work delivered the required results.

Before I dug into the code, though, I needed food and a cup of strong coffee. I wondered if I could convince Hardy's nano wave to produce a pizza for me.

PART SEVEN—CLEANUP

CHAPTER SIXTY-FIVE

With a sigh, Reginald dropped into the sand beside me. While he was still trying to find a comfortable sitting position, I leaned over and gave him a kiss.

He instantly gave up his efforts, placed one hand on the back of my head and kissed me back fervently. From the corner of my eye, I saw his member grow.

After a while, he let me go and took several deep breaths.

"Whew," I happily said.

"Each kiss with you is an event that deserves wholehearted devotion," he explained.

I glanced at his erection. "Do you want more devotion?"

"Honestly, I'm not in the mood for long foreplay."

"A quickie then." I pushed him on his back and squatted over him. I brushed his cock with my pubic hair three times before letting him inside me. It didn't take long before we both climaxed.

He came with another sigh, while I lustfully moaned when he discharged inside me.

We remained in that position — with me on top of him — for a while. After a while I leaned down and kissed him again. I felt him become hard again within a couple seconds.

"This could go on for hours," he said.

"But you've got something on your mind. Do you want to tell me what it is?"

"While we're like this? Oh, why not? I'm worried for Tess."

His hard-on lost some pressure. I pinched my pelvic muscles together to tease him. I wasn't ready to dismount yet.

"Ohh."

Reginald wasn't ready to let me go yet either. His pelvic muscles tensed, trying to give his cock a little more stimulation.

"Why are you worried about Tess?" I asked. "She's got her mission well under control. After all, we have three valuable newcomers."

"Three out of how many candidates? Plus, the mission doesn't seem to run easy all the time."

"Well, we knew it wouldn't be easy. The Cartel's broken up, but the individual regional groups don't like to give up their treasures."

"No, and that worries me. What if the experts don't want to leave?"

"Cooperative elements are not on Tess' list."

"No."

"She's good, Reginald. Trust her."

"Yes—aw, darn—I feel helpless."

His member went limp. He needed more stimulation. I moved up and down on him a bit.

"You're not helpless. Your contribution is valuable."

"Ahm."

"Your most important tool is your head, Reg. Most of the time, at least."

"Most of the time?"

"Right now, your most important tool is inside me. Come. Use it right."

CHAPTER SIXTY-SIX

Reginald stared out at the sea. The waves rolled over the reef, decorated with small white crests by the swelling wind. "I've been worrying about you, too."

"About me?"

"Yes. I've been worried since the message about your little trip arrived. That was the typical Jo. You can't patiently wait for us to check a new idea for potential weak spots. You just have to fly away with poorly adjusted emitters. Don't you?"

"You know I'm not really into theory."

He laughed. "Who developed the complete formula set for the Meier gravtunnel all alone within a few days? And who did the generator formula integration into the control software? If it were anyone else, they'd need months to develop and test a new release!"

"So what? I needed a few light months to test the release empirically."

"Sassy like a rude brat and unstoppable, too. I had once hoped that your Companion would slow you down a bit."

"There's a clear hierarchy in our relationship."

"Seems so."

I placed one hand on his upper leg but kept a careful distance from the sensitive inner side. I didn't want to stimulate him again.

"I'm used to acting independently. I've been on my own for so many years that it's simply normal for me to act once I'm ready. I gladly accept help — like in this case your program code — and I'm okay with asking for it, too. That's why we have pinboards. But when I recognize that an experiment will move us forward significantly, and it is worth the risks, I just act."

"Worth the risks? Your emitters could have burnt up, and you would've been stranded somewhere in outer space."

"So what? Worst case I'd have returned using the grav field drive. Regardless, I was prepared to die for this test."

"You'd have crawled back. How long would that have taken you? Thirty years, fifty, a hundred? You would have starved before returning!"

"I wouldn't have starved, Reg. As long as I don't have to do anything, I can last decades without food."

"So."

"I was thoroughly prepared, Reg. I didn't just patch something together and go off. I admit the code isn't pretty, but usable—in good conscience. But I did think about what else could go wrong, and the likelihood of those incidents occurring."

I looked at him, trying to see if I was putting his worries at ease.

"Why do you think I didn't start toward Centaur? I didn't want to rush into a neighboring sun in case my bubble worked too well. I was right. It did work too well, but nothing happened that I didn't already account for on my risk sheet."

"So you thought of everything."

"I also followed up on Francine's ideas."

"Oh. I didn't know she interfered."

"I asked her what I could've missed before the test. She gave me a few more good points before she transferred to the *Mayhem*."

"Mmmm." He leaned forward and took a handful of sand. "That's new. You asked someone beforehand—even though that someone had zero scientific knowledge or background."

"Francine isn't stupid, Reg. I have scientific knowledge myself. I wanted practical considerations. She provided the tip to shut a deuterium reserve away for emergencies. She advised me to seal the sanitary unit and to repack the flour provisions. She was the one who crawled into the central shaft to remove the starter batteries from the disruptor torpedoes."

"You had taken torpedoes along?"

"Sure. Imagine if we get a visitor and one of the few combat-ready spaceships is roaming our solar system's periphery — unarmed. That can't happen."

"No. Okay. Once again I find out that my Jo's got a much better grip on her tasks than an old chauvinist would like to admit. Still, it remains a fact that I was worried — even if unnecessarily."

"Yes." I took the hand away from his leg and caressed his cheek. "Thank you for that."

He smiled. "If I kiss you again, we'll never leave."

"Would that be so bad?"

"Not at all. Or yes, we'd miss dinner."

"That can't be." Nevertheless, I reached out with my other hand to caress his cock. "But we have a little time left. Put it in again."

CHAPTER SIXTY-SEVEN

A rmin nodded at Reginald and me when we entered the communication center. "Good evening, Jo. What new ideas do you bring us today?"

"Today? None. Reginald proposed we should clean up the pinboard and sort some questions out that are no longer relevant."

"Like, for example?"

"For example the *Ryūjin*. We don't need any more special solutions for a moon-sized spaceship if our Phoenix carriers are tunnel-capable already."

"I thought we agreed to continue the deployment of a carrier anyway?"

"Yes, sure, but it doesn't have to be that much bigger. Like an aircraft carrier perhaps, and we can judge the complexity of such a construction. A larger Phoenix might do."

Armin frowned. "And the latency times are manageable. Yes, you're right, that should make some topics obsolete."

Reginald clapped his hands. "Later, folks. Right now it's dinner time. After that, you may continue your discussions."

Thoughtfully, I gazed at the large remainder of our card collection. There were still so many topics!

"Now we know how to create a worm tunnel, but not where to go," Armin mused beside me. "Martha and Eduardo are still searching for the far point in our data—where the brown pest passed through."

Reginald tore another card off. "That's good, too." He

watched the writing. "Disguise. We no longer need to think about that."

"No?" I asked.

"No. It's already an effort to detect a nestle field beyond the Jupiter orbit or even behind the sun. Farther out, we have a hard time even though we know there's something."

He took a card and wrote something. Then he pinned *spy satellites* to the board. "It can't hurt if we stuff a sniffer, a transmitter, and a battery into a space probe and place a few of them farther out. That's cheap and could provide us with a decisive head start."

"If you think about it," Armin said. "A few years ago, it was a true challenge to send a probe to the outer planets. Now we're talking about it like it's a little excursion."

"Not quite as little."

"Aw, come on, Reginald. I've looked at the flight profiles. You accelerate one day at twenty g, fly three days at five percent c, and need one day for orbit approach. It will take five days to orbit Neptune. You could only dream of that back in the day."

"We could quite easily accelerate at two hundred g and fly twenty percent light," I added. "Then it's less than one-and-half days."

I expected objections, but to my surprise, Armin agreed.

"Right. The technology allows for that, but the risk of a collision with interstellar dirt and wearing down the satellite rises. Just wait to see what the *Mischief* examination tells us. We filed this method with the combat flight profiles. I strongly recommend flying like this only in emergencies."

Before I could object, he added, "Our time is precious, I know. But our pilots are more precious."

"I think you've got a point," I had to agree.

Reginald put one hand on my buttocks. "Come on, Jo. Scientists all over the world dreamed of a Mars mission. Before you, it would have taken them years to get to the Red Planet. Now they can plan a Mars station with two provisioning flights per month if we only give them one ship. Even a station on a Saturn moon is barely more expensive."

"Another topic for the board?"

"No. We needn't deal with that. The technical college on the mainland handle topics on the practical application of available technology."

"In that case, we can hand over the satellites, too. Send the card over."

"Even if it's a military topic?"

"First and foremost, it's a research topic. How many probes will we need to watch the entire system, and where should they go? What does an optimized deployment course look like? How often should the probes call home? Yes, okay, there's a military aspect, but no secret stuff. Give the boys and girls over there a thrilling and important goal that'll motivate them."

CHAPTER SIXTY-EIGHT

Walter took my second cup of coffee away from Nanette at the counter and brought it to me. He sat down next to me.

I suppressed a sigh.

"May I?" He seemed to be unaware of the fact that he'd already granted himself permission.

"You're lucky. Right now, I've got an open time slot for a Knight of the Order."

My irony was lost on him.

"Sorry to nag you at breakfast. I know you haven't had a minute to yourself since your return. You're a woman in high demand."

I took the cup into my hand, raised it, and breathed in the fresh smell of coffee. "Aside from my hobbies—that is, chasing terrorists, testing new aircraft, or dismantling Cartel-installed string puppet governments—I'm also the economic head of a research center plus teacher, researcher, and mascot. Plus, I'm also the military commander for Earth's Defence." I kept my many anonymously funded foundations to myself. "It's a miracle if I find three hours of sleep every other night."

"I'm sorry . . ."

"Come on. Spit it out. What have you got on your mind?"

"The Order and I, we want to support you as much as possible. So I wanted to ask you whether it's okay if I summon a few experts and we discuss how to employ the hypertunnel's tactical options. We can consult with your experts directly, so you don't have to worry about it."

"What kind of tactical options? Do you mean the gravtunnel when you say hypertunnel?"

He waved his right hand. "Hypertunnel, gravtunnel, whatever you call it. In any case, with it, you can quickly hop from one end to the other within the system—or arrive in the middle of the system behind the enemy like a surprise ambush. But I don't want to bother you with details—just tell me your top guy for that topic, and I'll pester him about it. We'll talk about how fast we can create such a tunnel, and whether we can change the destination until the last moment, and so on."

"Our expert for that topic is sitting beside you."

He fell mute, surprised.

"The creation of a Meier gravtunnel takes seconds, and you can change the destination until the last moment—or as fast as you can enter the new coordinates into the computer. The catch is that you must fly at a quarter light speed, and in the right direction. That takes about four hours from stand—or eight if you have to turn back. You can do such a maneuver at max twice during a battle, and then the spacecraft needs a dock."

"Can you change the direction of the tunnel while you are inside?" He raised his hand. "No, forget the question. I don't want to burden you with new stuff. May I take that along?"

I sipped my coffee. It was still a bit too hot. "Sure. Give it some thought. Ask Francine if you have questions about the application of the Meier gravtunnel. Your questions are interesting. If I had the time, I'd think about it."

"Not so important."

"No. Indeed not. A change of direction would only make sense if you could gain new insights inside the tunnel. But you're flying practically blind and deaf."

"Not entirely." He smiled. "If your opponent observes your transition into the tunnel and draws conclusions about your destination from it, surprising him by arriving elsewhere would be quite useful."

I turned the cup in my hand once around its axis but gazed through it. "You've got a point there. Write a card."

Chapter Sixty-nine

With the rest of my coffee, I walked over to one of our communication computers, sat down before it and logged in. That was a clear signal to everyone — do not disturb.

I didn't have a private e-mail address. If I did, my inbox would probably be flooded with mail. When I did receive mail, it was forwarded from the University's general e-mail address. My personal messages were usually from personal contacts or those with a special code that I had defined myself.

This time, I found both kinds of mail.

One was from Rashid. The Secretary for Interstellar Defence urgently invited me to a meeting with the newly installed UN Defence Council — preferably in New York, but they'd come to any place determined by me.

I thought about it briefly. It was afternoon in New York already. It took two hours to fly there, and I'd arrive in the early evening — too close to set up a meeting. I replied that I'd arrive at noon on the following day and asked him to organize a landing permit for Downtown Manhattan Heliport.

The other mail originated from a network of surveillance programs, which I used to keep track of my foundations' transactions.

According to the e-mail, someone had tried to re-route money into his own pocket. The concerned person obviously didn't know whose money he was taking.

Zoe, I could use some help here, I thought. I carried the *memories* of the most skilled hacker of all times in my head — that had to be good for something!

It had at least been good enough to install my surveillance programs. Now the knowledge I inherited from Zoe could help me substantiate or invalidate my initial suspicion.

Nanette replaced my almost empty coffee cup with a fresh one.

"Thanks."

The money flowed from my foundation's account to an account owned by a company connected to one of my trustees. Three days later, there was a larger private withdrawal from the company's account. Two days later, someone deposited the money into another bank account. My trustee surely thought I wouldn't know about this secret account.

He should've paid more attention to his contract. The financial affairs of trustees working for my foundations were always made transparent to me if the foundations' interests *could* be affected.

Another paragraph said that the founder was entitled to check their compliance with contractual regulations. Accordingly, I was entitled to check my foundations' finances, and — once there was any suspicion of fraud — I could investigate all the bank accounts related to any trustees involved in the case. I did just that, and the evidence was ironclad.

Independent of a court investigation, a trustee liable for personal misbehavior could lose all his assets. I had caught him with his hands in the cookie jar, and now he had to pay his dues. Within a few minutes, I channeled all his liquid funds back to the foundation, seized his tangible assets, and revoked his access to the foundation's assets. After that, I sent him a notice of termination. I also informed all of the foundation's officials that this trustee was no longer allowed to perform any role.

When all of that was done, I took a sip of my coffee and sent the information of the entire operation to a lawyer's office, which could take care of possible juristic consequences. I didn't worry about that, though.

"Can I do anything for you?" Nanette asked.

"Thank you, but no—or yes. Can you relay to whoever is on duty that I need the Taipan tonight?"

"Sure."

Nanette left, and I briefly stared at the screen before me, then typed another message to Rashid. After recent developments, it was only appropriate for me to pay a visit to the different units I was commanding.

CHAPTER SEVENTY

The approach to New York, between the Verrazano-Narrows Bridge's arches up the Hudson, offered me a grand view of the Statue of Liberty, Manhattan's southern tip, and the bridges across the East River. The heliport at Manhattan's western shore came into sight much too soon. I decided not to take the extra round over the city to be polite.

I parked the Taipan gently without it rocking or shaking. The marshaller gave me a thumbs up and stuck the beacon under his arm. He turned around and hurried toward the flat pavilion, where three people in thick coats were waiting in front of a black stretch limousine and two black Martians.

I knew one of the three men. The mayor of New York had personally appeared to welcome me. I was surprised they were there, as I was over one hour early for my appointment with the United Nations. I wondered how long they'd stood waiting for me. Well, at least, they would spare me a taxi tour.

My plane trembled a bit when I shut the systems down. As soon as I opened the canopy, the wind tore at me. I pushed myself up and jumped out of the cockpit. I waited until the canopy was closed before I ambled over to the three waiting men.

My black combat suit didn't protect me from the frosty temperatures, but I was all too familiar with winter in New York. A little Dragon power warmed me from the inside.

"Welcome to New York, Protectress," said the man I had learned to know as the *Fool* when the city was firmly in the Syndicate's grip. He greeted me and reached out a hand.

I ignored the hand, hugged him, and placed a kiss on his cheek. "Hello. Please don't be so formal."

"Pardon an old fool." He winked at me and pointed at the limousine. "Would you like a ride?"

"Out of pity for your employees, yes." I smiled at one of them. The corner of his mouth twitched, despite his professionally-distanced face.

Something was wrong. One glance outside the window confirmed my suspicion. "This is not the way to the UNO."

Our small convoy rolled up 11th Avenue, occasionally interrupted by a red light. Otherwise, the ride went by smoothly.

"You're right. We have a little time left. There's something I want to show you."

"Okay. Is there a problem?"

"Not at all."

After a few turns, we approached Verdi Square between 72nd and 73rd street. I had met the *Fool* for the first time in this square.

Back then, he really behaved like a fool—with long hair and a guitar in hand. He used to play satirical songs about the Syndicate, which hardly anyone listened to in this square. Now, he had no guitar, but many people crowded around the square.

As soon as our limousine stopped at the curb in Broadway, a uniformed policeman hurried toward us. That stirred unpleasant memories in me, even though I knew the criminal cops of the past had all been relieved.

"You can't stop here," the policeman told the driver through the opened side window.

My host leaned forward. "I think we can, officer."

The policeman peeked into the back. "Oh, good morning, Mr. Mayor. Please, drive on. It's hard enough to keep the traffic flowing with the people here already."

"It's not about me, officer. It's about our guest."

Finally the policeman took note of me.

"Velvet?" he uttered, surprised. "Oh. Of course."

He pulled his head out of the car. Shortly afterward, a whistle blew where the man in blue stood. Three minutes later, all of Broadway was blocked off and the people around the square were held back.

"Please free the square," the policemen commanded the crowd. "Thank you."

Sometimes grumbling, but mostly curious, the people withdrew. Finally, the small square was empty.

The mayor looked at me and pointed at the door. "Please."

Surrounded by two bodyguards, he led me to the square and pointed at the bronze statue of a short woman squatting on the ground before one of the park benches. I knew the woman's features were my own.

"There were long discussions about what a memorial for you should look like," he explained. "A large faction vouched for a gigantic statue with a torch in your hand at the southern end of Central Park. It was supposed to be modeled after Lady Liberty because you gave us back our freedom. Others wanted to build a memorial wall with a chained fighter breaking her chains."

The mayor raised his palms. "I have to admit that I liked the heroic symbolism in both those designs. However, those who claimed to know you better favored this design. Their argument was that you're a modest human being in accounts. They said that you always stressed the contributions of each individual. We thought the modesty expressed in this statue would do you and your claims justice."

He seemed to identify himself with this *We* strongly.

I circled the squatting woman once. There was no pedestal, but only a shining brass ring set into the pavement with some text written on it.

Velvet — Protectress Johanna Meier, PoOoDL — Liberator of New York — Sunday, December 9th, 2063 — The individual's courage counts — Walk tall!

"Remember your speech at your award ceremony? I admit, we somewhat shortened the text here."

I ignored him. Instead, I bent down to a small engraving on a brass badge that someone had later added in front of my crossed legs inside the official ring.

For Johanna, we will do everything. *The New Yorkers.*

I didn't have to ask what *everything* meant. I squatted down before the statue, unintentionally copying its posture, and gazed up at the mayor.

"That's not official," he said. "During the first two, three days, there were a few people who removed the badge. The next morning, it was back. Once I learned about it, I gave the order to leave it alone."

I looked at the people surrounding the square. The first people who were shooed away from this square had understood why the area was being blocked.

I heard whispers, "Velvet."

"The Protectress."

"It's her."

"She squatted down."

"Did she cry?"

A few people started clapping, then more joined them. The applause spread like a forest fire.

What could I do? I rose, spun with my arms spread out, then I bowed deeply.

I stayed like that for a long moment before standing up and looking the mayor directly in the eyes. "I think we have some time left for a late breakfast."

"Yes, sure. Do you have a preferred destination?"

"How about Joe's at the corner of 74th Street and Amsterdam Avenue?"

"Good idea."

"I'd like to walk the few steps there."

He briefly glanced at his two personal security men. "I guess in the Protectress' presence I'm safe, guys. Follow us in the cars, won't you?"

Chapter Seventy-One

The mayor pointed at the open door of Joe's Deli, and I went ahead. The proprietor was pouring coffee for a customer when we entered. He glanced up at us, then glanced up again. When he recognized us, a dash of hot coffee hit his left hand, and he quickly placed the cup and jug down.

"Feed me to the Jelly!"

"Only after I get my coffee, Joe."

He hastily cleaned his hand with his apron before going around his counter and wrapping his long arms around me.

I returned the hug and held him tight. He trembled and sobbed.

By now, the other guests had noticed that something uncommon was happening. Okay, of course, they recognized their mayor, but he just sat down at a free table and watched Joe and me.

After a long hug, Joe finally let me go. He pushed me away at arm's length and looked into my eyes. I returned his gaze, even if I had to twist my head far back to do it.

"What do you want? Once up and down the menu?"

"Just scrambled eggs with fried potatoes and bacon, please."

"In a moment. Coffee with it?"

"Gladly."

"That's on the house. No argument. This is a question of honor." He turned around. "Mr. Mayor, eggs, and coffee, too?"

The addressee nodded. "Thank you, yes."

Joe pushed his staff outside to the street with a large coffee jug and a pile of cups for the bodyguards. Then he tackled the stove to prepare our meals.

One of his guests at the next table leaned forward and dared to ask, "Hello. I'm Brian of the *Examiner*. Say, what brings Velvet into this deli? You guys seem to know each other very well?"

"Oh, hello, Brian. Yes, we've met before. You could say the resistance started here, in this deli."

"Not in the Guggenheim?"

"That was the *official* start, Brian. Here in Joe's Deli, Trevor of the *Gotham Chronicle* started to spread the news of Velvet's visit to New York. Did you know Trevor? In the past, he always came here."

"Trevor? No. Never met him. Perhaps I should interview him. The *Chronicle,* you said?"

"He died during the liberation. Like so many others."

"Oh." Then his journalistic ambition awoke within him. "What brings you to New York, *Protectress?*"

CHAPTER SEVENTY-TWO

Rashid welcomed me in the hallway before the conference rooms in the United Nations main building. My black suit didn't fit in here, I mused upon sight of his pretty white-red-green-golden Arabic robe. My wardrobe was too reminiscent of war.

"Hello, Johanna. You're here early, I have to tell you something." He fell silent, and the worry on his face gave way to a fake smile.

"Oh, hello, Mr. Miller. May I introduce to you the Imperatrix Aurea Johanna Meier. Johanna, this is Abraham Miller, the American representative in the council."

"Hello," I said in a friendly voice and reached out a hand.

"Hello," he replied curtly. He shook my hand briefly. "I assume we all must be grateful that you finally found time for us."

"Of course, I gave the Secretary's request for an appointment the highest priority," I said with a nod toward Rashid.

"Well, the council was installed a few weeks ago," Miller drilled on. "So we can hardly ask for the military commandant of Earth's forces to find her way to us immediately to give a full account."

"At the time of installment—which I wasn't aware of in advance, by the way—I was on a test mission in space," I explained in a matter-of-fact voice. "If I hadn't returned early due to an unexpectedly successful test, the council would have had to be patient for a few more weeks. You can't just take a taxi out there, you know?"

"We'll talk about that," he insisted.

"We shouldn't keep the others waiting," Rashid proposed and pointed at a half-open door. I heard quiet conversations—mainly about winter-related impediments in air traffic—coming from the other side of the door.

We entered, and the conversations fell mute. The Sheikh introduced me to the other people present in order.

Lasse Jorgensson from Trondheim in Norway represented the European bloc. With his short straw-blond hair, he looked like he was in his mid-forties. However, I calculated that he was in his late fifties, due to the wrinkles around his eyes.

Sergej Markoff from Moscow attended the council for the Russians, although he officially represented *northern Asia*. He had no top hair left and wore a short silver-gray chin beard instead.

Wei Ching from Peking, China, represented the southern Asian region. I couldn't instantly tell whether the greased black hair on top of his friendly round face was his natural hair or a toupee. In the end, I opted for the former.

"I'm the Kiwi," Jack Turner from Wellington in New Zealand introduced himself. The slender giant with the short black curls represented Australia and Oceania.

Sheikh Hassan al Muktur looked almost like a relative of Rashid with his turban but came from Saudi Arabia. He gave my figure-hugging suit a brief, disapproving glare. He pointed out he represented the Arabic-Muslim world.

A chubby woman with dark complexion in a dark green robe had remained in the back until then. "Call me Nellie," she demanded. Nellie Okonambe from Johannesburg, South Africa, represented her continent.

Who represented South America, then?

I kept that question to myself. Seven people were probably too many for a council that had to make quick decisions in a crisis.

CHAPTER SEVENTY-THREE

I found out not much later that seven people were *seven* too many. I figured out that politics wasn't my world — at least the kind of politics these people performed.

Lasse, Jack, and Nellie were quite nice. I could imagine joining them for a beer if the conversation didn't touch politics. They were well-versed politicians, that is, they didn't make binding statements, agreed even to the most simple questions only with reservations, and challenged everything that wasn't pure math, so they challenged practically everything.

Sergej and Wei were a bit difficult. It took a lot to get an understandable statement from them if they spoke up at all.

Sheikh Hassan met Nellie and me with open misogyny — if he took note of us at all, he did it with a disrespectful smile or raised eyebrows.

Mr. Miller was the worst of them all. He didn't deserve to be addressed by his first name, regardless of the fact that he strictly refused to tolerate such ingratiatory attempts. I wondered what had made the Americans send him to this council before me.

Quite obviously — and only in this point did all seven members agree — this council regarded itself as a control-and-direct board for Rashid and me, and thus they believed that they had authority over me. So far, I hadn't commented on that. From Rashid's occasional, politically sensible remarks, I deducted that we might need these people in the future and shouldn't put them off. I wasn't sure how much tolerance I could muster, though.

"There's also the question," Miller said, beginning his next tirade, "of how we want to keep the different units under control after we've exclusively equipped them with all these marvel weapons. Who can restrain such a cocky fighter pilot?"

"Me" I replied with ease.

"We should trust your word on that? We should trust the word of a young, inexperienced woman?"

That was enough. I stood up. Rashid made a covert defensive gesture, but it was too late.

"You can all trust me with one thing. You can trust me to be standing in the front ranks. Once the next interstellar attack comes, I will be risking my life, while you're sitting in your safe bunkers. If you don't trust me, then this council can't exist. Is that clear? And in this case, there are only two legit answers—yes or no. So?"

"Under the condition . . ." Lasse began.

"Stop. No reservations, no conditions, no restrictions. No back door. Yes or no?"

"Yes."

"I can't decide that alone," Miller said.

"That's a no. If you can't even decide this matter on your own, you're out. This assembly has no use for people who can't make their own judgments."

"But . . ."

"There's the door!" I thundered at him and pointed at the door with an outstretched finger. Not entirely by chance, I let a long golden claw poke out at the tip of my fingers.

"That's a misunderstanding!"

"It's not. I asked for a yes or no. A first-year pupil can understand that. Out."

"That's not for you to decide."

That was his biggest mistake. Before he knew it, I had grabbed him by the collar and crotch, kicked the door open with my foot, and thrown him out.

Then I turned around and watched the remaining partici-
pants while the noise-proof door slowly closed behind me. Six
of them stared at me in disbelief. Only Rashid smiled openly.

"I can, and I will enforce my decisions. Clear?"

Jack smiled now, too. "I trust you. Yes."

Nellie agreed as well.

"Sergej?"

"Yes."

My gaze fell on the Chinese, and his gaze focused on my
golden claw. "Long," his lips formed. Then he quietly said,
"Yes."

That left only Hassan. He managed a thin smile, too. "Yes."

I let the claw disappear. "Good. Back to the facts. Miller
was right about one thing. We are placing a significant
amount of power into the hands of individual people. We are
doing that because they will need that power to protect our
people and our world. We very much hope that they live up
to the trust we've bestowed upon them."

My pause gave them time to understand, and it gave me
time to consider my next words.

"Remember that these people, in turn, trust us to make the
decisions that will prepare them in the best possible way for
a life-or-death fight — a fight not all of them will survive. Our
soldiers must bear this residual risk to their lives as we must
realize that we will make mistakes. We may place our trust on
the wrong people. Should such a case arise, I will, of course,
stand between these misled people and my *protected,* as I did
in the past. If anyone has any doubts about my *experience* in
this field, they are welcome to watch my battle in New York.
There is a video of our fight in Central Park. Or you could ask
one of the New Yorkers who was there back then."

Now I focused on Hassan. "And don't be deceived by my
juvenile appearance. I *remember* the third crusade and all the

pain and injustice done in the name of religion back then. I *remember* how Jerusalem looked in the past, and I *remember* many proud and brave warriors who died by my sword because my survival appeared so much more valuable than theirs. That's my treasure trove of experience, even if it was the body of Zoe's mother collecting these experiences. I also *remember* the Invasion, where I had ventured out with eight companions to conquer the enemy mothership, even if it was Zoe's body collecting these experiences. Think about that before anyone calls me *inexperienced* again."

Rashid cleared his throat.

"One moment. To avoid any misunderstandings, I want to be clear to all of you. I don't want to have a board of yea-sayers around me. I can err. Disagree with me, talk back hard. But leave my gender and my integrity out of it. If you can't do that, at least wrap your insults a bit more kindly than this donkey Miller."

This time, even Hassan's smile seemed to be genuine, but it disappeared with my next words.

"Oh yes. Another clarification. As Imperatrix Aurea, I *am* the supreme commander. This board will not challenge my authority openly or indirectly, or I will challenge this board as I just demonstrated with Miller."

Now I nodded at Rashid. "I will briefly confer in private with Mr. Secretary. I hope you take the time to discuss my undiplomatic behavior without having to watch your words."

CHAPTER SEVENTY-FOUR

Without saying a word, Rashid led me to an adjacent conference room. When the door shut behind him, he turned to me. He was pressing his lips together, and his eyes were glaring.

"I'm sorry," I spoke up first. "I know I didn't make your work easier. We still need these people, and I may have offended them. You're angry now, and I understand that."

I shook my head. "I just couldn't allow them to have the wrong first impression of me. I'm a ruler, and I expect some show of respect."

"Of course you do. I'm not angry at you. I'm angry at Miller and the idiot who sent him. You didn't have to boot Miller so literally, though. I'm also angry at myself because I allowed this to escalate."

He waved toward the assembly room. "I shouldn't have confirmed the date before aligning the members. Now we'll just have to see how they take it. Some of our discussions may be more difficult now, but some of it will be easier because you set a few cornerstones. Miller wasn't the only one who wanted to gain influence over you through this board."

"Hassan."

"Yes, of course. His view on women is a bit old-fashioned. But he's intelligent and quite open to pragmatic solutions. On the other hand, the Chinese representative can be quite difficult."

"If he causes trouble, tell me. Then I'll transform into a Dragon. I believe that's his weak point."

The Sheikh smirked. "That's a different kind of diplomacy."

"I can't acquire a taste for this wriggling back and forth," I admitted. "If it goes too far, I need to speak up."

"That's not diplomatic."

"As my predecessor once said, the humans must get along with me for the next thousand years. I only have to abide these people for a few decades."

Rashid frowned.

"Nor can we collaborate that long, although I truly regret that."

"Thank you. Let's go back. We still have a few substantial topics to discuss."

CHAPTER SEVENTY-FIVE

Our second round began with a series of more or less friendly, but *political* assurances from the remaining members. They were interested in constructive collaboration and of course would never doubt my competencies again. Hassan and Sergej were so tame, it was as if they'd taken soothing drugs. Both insinuated that they were not truly happy with Miller.

"Just talk straight," I asked them. "He was an idiot. An ambitious idiot, but still an idiot. You, on the other hand, have your political and your personal agenda, but you're smart enough to recognize what's at stake."

I let the shock on their face die down before I continued speaking. "I also think you understand that I'm neither in the mood nor have time to waste on political games. My only concern is humanity's defense. Whether one or another makes a profit from that is secondary to me."

Some tried to suppress a frown, some slowly nodded. "In other words, as long as I get the results I need, I don't care about the political chess moves among yourselves. I won't interfere with that. Moreover, I promise that anything we discuss in this circle remains in this circle — except for the decisions we write down and the tasks we distribute. Okay?"

The six men and one woman looked at each other. Finally, Sheikh Hassan spoke up. "We'll see how we can work with that. For now, we thank you for your openness. That will take some getting used to."

I only nodded and glanced at Rashid. He began with a

summary of our most recent successes. Nellie's first question proved that he was only partially successful.

"I'm sorry. Perhaps it's due to my language skills, but these wormholes and tunnels are beyond me."

To me, it seemed as if the men fared the same, but Nellie didn't lose anything by admitting her ignorance.

"I'll try to explain it simply," I began. "Since Albert Einstein — you know the name? Good — okay, since Einstein, we know, or believe we know, that the energy needed to accelerate a mass to light speed is quite high. That's E equals m times c squared, okay? We had to provide fossil fuel with a mass greater than zero to accelerate a spaceship toward light speed. This was impossible, until now."

Everyone in the room had a confused expression on their faces. "Too complicated? Then let me put it differently. To make your car that fast you'd have to fill in more fuel than the weight of your car — including fuel. That just can't work."

I glanced around. "Nevertheless, three times in the past, we've had travelers from other stars who traveled faster than light. First came the Dragons, then came the Jellies, and the last was a strange substance with the ability to mimic other life forms. This weird brown pest was able to conquer a Jelly mothership. Because of this, I believe that this creature is more powerful and dangerous to us than the Jellies put together. However, I digress — all these travelers used wormholes to enter our system."

I tore the first sheet off a notepad and held it up. "Let's say this is space. From one end to the other is a long way."

I folded two diagonally opposite corners together and held the sheet up again.

"Now it looks like the way from one corner to the other would be quite short. Only the fabric of space — the paper — is still blocking the way."

I pierced the paper with a claw. "But if you make a hole,

you can take a shortcut. That still costs a tremendous lot of energy, but it's much cheaper than the conventional journey if you only know how it works. We call this kind of shortcut a wormhole because you eat your way like a worm through the paper."

Now Nellie nodded. "I think I understand so far. What's new now?"

I showed my claw. "The old method is quite brutal. You tear a coarse hole into the fabric of space, which costs a lot of energy and causes a lot of side effects. Among other things, it's quite unhealthy to linger in the vicinity of a nascent hole."

"How unhealthy?" Lasse asked.

"Any matter in a radius of several light seconds is destroyed. Molecules become atoms, and those are dissembled as well. There wouldn't even be dust from a planet left."

"Oh."

"Exactly. I found this method quite rough, too. So I thought about it and found another, more elegant solution that works with much less energy and hardly any side effects. The paper remains intact, so to speak. At no point in time is there an entire hole. Instead, the spaceship winds its way through the layers of paper, pushes them a little out of the way and allows them to quickly slip back into their original structure after passing through."

"You thought that up? All alone?" Jack asked.

"Yes."

"How many people on Earth could have done that, too?"

"With the respective education in Dragon technology? A few dozen would have the necessary knowledge, but only a handful of people have the right specialization. Besides me, there might be two or three people capable of completing this concept if they took a few years' time. I was a little faster because I can keep complex interrelations in my mind better due to my *memory*."

"Two or three . . . in a few years," Jack repeated and gazed at Hassan. "I don't think we're in the position to appropriately appreciate this level of scientific competence. None of us."

Hassan bowed his head. "I agree."

That went down smoothly. But Nellie's question wasn't answered yet, so I continued, "Let's put the scientific foundations aside and focus on the consequences. With a wormhole generator like those the Jellies have, you can punch a hole into space and fly through it. Due to the side effects, you must keep a very considerable distance from the Sun—about twenty-one days of flight, as we've calculated. You can do this only three or four times before even the energy reserves of a Jelly mothership are entirely exhausted. A tunnel field, on the other hand, can be created a few minutes away from Earth—and the power of a little Barracuda suffices to travel several light years. So, instead of taking years to prepare for a journey to the moon—like we did with the Apollo rocket—we only need a couple of days. It would be like planning a short road trip from the east to the west coast instead of a space mission."

"Based on your analogy, our options are more flexible by orders of magnitude," Jack concluded.

"Correct," I agreed. "Okay, that was the very first attempt. We still need some fine tuning. The most important thing to consider is the wear on the ship's aggregates. Sticking with our comparison, imagine you need a new set of tires every two hundred kilometers, and there are no garages along your way. But you can't take that many spare wheels along, either. My colleagues on the island are analyzing these effects."

"So the problem can be solved?"

"The collected data must be processed, and the technical parameters must be adjusted accordingly. That takes time, but we don't expect any big unwanted surprises."

Now Rashid spoke up. "About one year ago, briefly after

my assignment to the office of Secretary for Interstellar Defence, I asked Johanna as Dragon empress and leader of the only relevant research institute to evaluate a reconnaissance mission."

Rashid's words were met with curiosity. The council members didn't seem to have a clue where Rashid was heading. "To prepare ourselves for a possible attack, I deemed it indispensable to procure more intelligence on our opponent. To that end, we needed two things — the origin of the enemy and an option to travel there."

At that, the council members nodded in assent. "If I interpret the current information correctly, the second problem is principally solved. It's only about dealing with the wear-off problem and planning the actual reconnaissance mission. Correct?"

"More or less," I admitted. "We had planned to build a mothership for such a journey."

"But now it seems as if we wouldn't necessarily need a capital ship — at least not for a reconnaissance mission, correct?"

"Correct. A Phoenix-class ship would be sufficient. The capital ship has its advantages in combat against opponents of comparable sizes."

"But even a Barracuda would be enough to sneak into a foreign system, correct? Small enough that the enemy might even fail to notice it — not considering its detectability?"

"Correct," I agreed. "That should be calculated, but the assumption is plausible."

"We had originally planned a pure reconnaissance mission," Rashid explained. "We wanted to drop a few rovers for analysis — no Dragon technology, only pre-invasion-technology so that the enemy couldn't draw conclusions from it."

Everyone in the room was silent, listening intently to Rashid. So he continued speaking. "Our technicians came up with ideas right away. They concluded that we'd need landing rockets, parachutes, etc. They also raised some questions. We will need to know the surface of the enemy's planet and the level of gravity to expect. We also wondered about the atmosphere's composition and the climate of their world. We postulate a surface that can be walked on, since the Jellies would've had a hard time otherwise, and an environment where this strange organism can survive, but we come out blank concerning anything else about their planet. We need to know more before we can send even a probe down. That's why we want to send a scout."

Several council members nodded. I did, too.

"There is a catch." Rashid went on, "There is the risk of detection. If the scout is spotted, that could warn the enemy and give them clues about our technology. If the scout is caught, it could give the enemy the opportunity to study and replicate this technology — or worse, gain access to our data and Earth's location. Therefore, the scout must be equipped with a self-destruction mechanism."

Several council members raised their hands. Before he opened the round for discussion, Rashid concluded his presentation. "Nevertheless, I think the possible intelligence gain by such a reconnaissance mission more than justifies the risk. What remains is the discovery of the fact that such a scout is technically possible. But right now that's purely a theory, because we don't know yet where to send such a scout."

"No," I agreed. "That's the search for the needle in the haystack, especially as the last wormhole was hard to find."

"It would be easier to pinpoint which hole the Jelly mothership originally came through," Rashid added, and I stared at him. Yes. You only had to search those systems for a pattern.

CHAPTER SEVENTY-SIX

I had barely reached my hotel room when the telephone rang. I hurried over and answered the call.

"Office of the president. Please hang on." There was a click. Then I heard the voice of the current American president.

"*Protectress* Johanna, thank you very much for giving me a moment of your time. Are you alone?"

"Yes. What can I do for the American president?"

"Nothing. You are actively helping me already. I must apologize," he said with surprising frankness. "There are certain domestic political problems which I must negotiate with the opposition. Lately, these problems concerned the candidate nominated for the UN Council for Interstellar Defence. I presume I can't persuade you to reverse his boot?"

I had to grin. "No, sorry. The boot indeed happened and can't be undone. You may tell your opposition that I regard the sending of such an idiot as a deliberate and severe insult and that I expect compensation."

"What sort of compensation?" he asked back. Apparently, he didn't think my demand was amiss.

"Send a member of the Order to the council, or someone with proven scientific competence. I believe you can find someone with one or both of these criteria whom your opposition can't reject."

"He has to represent the American interests, too."

"If he has some brains in his head, he'll quickly spot the political schemes. According to my judgment, you can trust Rashid to keep a balance of interest between all the parties

230

involved. Tell that to your man."

"I will do that. How's it going otherwise?"

"I'm worried. It seems the Jellies aren't the only threat out there, and we're far from prepared to reliably counter a new invasion. While I'm trying to find a solution to this problem, the council warns me about soldiers who could misuse their new tools."

The president remained silent.

"At home, I have the same problem with my students. I have no way to discern which of them might covertly work for a different party. Then, there are the unknown terrorists who tried to steal Dragon technology a few times. In other words, while we're trying to erect a wall against the next storm surge with bare hands, all the people who'd like to backstab us are positioning their forces."

"Oh dear. What can I do?"

"Talk with your people—the CIA or the NSA. Tell them to keep their eyes and ears open. Perhaps they should even talk to the Russians."

"To the Russians?"

"They can say it was my idea. If you find something, send Walter a note. He can have a look around on the island and knows my people well. I won't be mad at him for being vigilant. Understood?"

"Understood. I'll pull my strings."

"Thanks."

"No. I should thank *you*. By the way, my office knows I'll tear the head off anyone who doesn't patch you through instantly. Okay?"

"If you don't mean that literally, yes."

He laughed. "That's the little difference between the two of us."

CHAPTER SEVENTY-SEVEN

The rough, barren mountain landscape of the southern Sinai Peninsula stretched out for kilometers in all directions beneath me. Straight ahead, I recognized the distinctive tip of Gebel Katherîna, the tallest mountain on the peninsula, which stood more than two-thousand six-hundred meters high.

My destination lay near the foot of the mountain — Saint Catherine's Monastery, one of the world's oldest Christian monasteries.

At the moment, it was no more than a landmark, a place where I could park my Taipan until the end of my mission.

I jumped out of the cockpit, then waited patiently for the canopy to close and the computer to confirm that everything was secure. Then I looked around.

The first three kilometers around the monastery were regarded as neutral territory. I was safe here. That wouldn't last long, though.

Again, I ran through my route in my mind. There were many options to travel from here to Dahab at the Gulf of Aqaba, sixty kilometers away on the map, as the crow flies. The road a few kilometers north of me was no doubt the most comfortable route. This road — more precisely, its southern edge — marked the boundary of the legitimate mission area, but it was off limits. I wasn't supposed to swim along the coast, either.

So everything boiled down to a longer mountain hike, with the minor condition that I not be caught. After a brief orientation — and I didn't sense any active fusion reactor except for the one in my plane — I jogged away heading southeast.

From the moment I arrived, the hunt on me was open, and if even one opponent picked up my tracks, I'd have an entire regiment of armor suits, totaling four-hundred-eighty-six tandem couples, on my heels.

Rashid had passed on my request for a meeting to his daughter. Fatima had called back before my departure from New York.

"Hello, Protectress. *The Secretary told me you are going to visit your infantry unit."*

"Correct. I'm always very busy, but since I'm no longer cruising beyond the inner planets, I have no good excuse to postpone this task any longer. I know you did a good job with your instructions and still do, but it's just good manners to meet the people personally, meet your deputies and battalion leaders and get my impression on their performance."

"Your visit comes at a somewhat inconvenient time, as we're currently doing an operation at southern Sinai. That's why I wasn't able to reply until now. We were in the country for the past three days."

"A Sinai operation? Then let's make that a test."

"A test?"

"A hunt. I'm the prey. If I can't make it from the heart of the peninsula to the coast within four days or you catch me, you win. Or, if I reach the agreed upon destination, then I win."

"Four days? The peninsula's quite large."

"It will only take me a day to cross if you don't stop me. You won't be able to, but you can try."

"You make crossing the peninsula sound like a walk in the park."

"We'll see if I'm wrong."

"Is that a challenge? Okay. I'll make sure you don't get bored. Any rules?"

"No rules, except for the boundaries. Oh, and you must protect the civil population from the aggressor, which in this case would be me."

"Would you risk the life of civilians for a test?"

"Of course not. But if you use your people as a shield against me, that wouldn't be just a foul for the exercise, but reason for disciplinary action. Clear?"

"Clear."

There were no rules, except for the boundaries. Of course, I couldn't fly my Taipan to the destination either. I could only rely on myself and my surroundings to complete the mission.

This mission was not difficult for *Velvet*. After all, I was used to infiltrating areas guarded by armor suits. I could disguise myself. I could reduce my heat radiation, which required less effort since it was quite hot during the days here. I could move like a cat.

The distance was a problem. Sixty kilometers in a straight line meant a lot of climbing up and down the mountains, especially if I didn't want to make detours. I couldn't keep up perfect invisibility for sixty kilometers. That was simply too expensive.

So I helped myself to a basic camouflage pattern matching the surroundings, and used the landscape as additional cover.

Fatima didn't have much time to deploy her people, but armor suits were fast and efficient. Plus, they didn't have to worry about being spotted.

In their place, I'd have circled the area around the monastery with a few units to intercept me, while the search radius was still small. I would assign a second contingent to cover the destination. The remaining regiment, I would distribute across key positions all over the mission area. There would be soldiers posted on peaks to guard several mountain crests, valley junctions, and summits. To me, this meant there were a lot of spots to avoid.

If only I could manage to get past the first perimeter, I'd be fine. Three kilometers radius didn't reflect a large area, and there were some places in the mountains where the monastery could be observed.

For an armor suit, a three or five kilometer line-of-sight was nothing. That was clearly outside the linear cannons' effective range, but the visor could still indicate conspicuous movements at this distance.

I did not take my mission lightly. From time to time, I stopped and tried to sense the fusion backpacks' characteristic stray emissions. I did this in vain, but I remained vigilant.

My caution proved necessary. I had left the neutral area two kilometers behind and begun to climb a steep and stony mountain slope when I heard a bang and saw a rock a few meters upslope explode into small shards. Only a linear cannon at full power could cause such an effect.

So, they shot live bullets at me. Fatima had kept her promise. This would in no way be boring!

CHAPTER SEVENTY-EIGHT

M y *Analogy* helped me locate the shooter's position quickly—the rock shards' trajectory was the starting point for that. He sat below a peak in the same mountain range that I was climbing.

Across this distance, he had to shoot at full power so his steel bullets would fly straight and not drop to the ground after half the distance. It was bad luck for me, since such projectiles could penetrate my reinforced skin as easily as they could crush rocks. Each hit was potentially lethal!

I improved my camouflage to full invisibility, checked the area, and jumped into a better-protected position.

It wouldn't be difficult for me to find a well-covered route to this shooter and take him out. If I did, it would prove to him and all other suits in the area that he had indeed spotted me. If he was certain that he spotted me, he would have turned all the rocks in the surrounding area into fragments already.

It was possible, though, that another soldier had a better angle to take me out and was just trying to spot me. In a veil of dust and rocks, that would be hard to accomplish.

Working on this assumption, I soon found another shooter sitting on a rock. His camouflage was almost too perfect, only not good enough for Dragon eyes. A third shooter was waiting for his chance to strike, but his suit was running on its batteries to avoid the typical fusion reactor emissions. *Sorry, boys and girls, this party takes place without me.*

I found myself a different way up the slope and took my

leave.

Now that I could tell what kind of positions the armor suits preferred, I managed to escape the first search perimeter without trouble and covered the next thirty kilometers un-challenged. Along the way, I rarely met a scout team — it was a damn large area for so few soldiers, after all. They could try to guess my route, and the rest was basic statistics.

My mishap was owed to statistics as well. I was just in the process of sneaking past another team in full camouflage when a piece of rock already weakened by erosion broke un-der my feet. A bold jump carried me to safety from the first salvo. Then the other half of the tandem couple of armor suits started shooting at me, too. He didn't aim at the places I could have been, though. Instead, he let his underarm cannons wan-der very quickly in circles shooting at the surrounding area. The first shooter complemented the pattern, restricting me.

I had to be pretty darn fast to get through this steel rain without being hit. The way they were tightening the circles, my odds dropped with each fraction of a second. To make matter worse, I hardly had a chance to predict their varying patterns. This was bad.

But their linear cannons needed power — a *lot* of power, more than their spare batteries could provide. There were no rules. This was life or death. So I sent a shower of control quarks in their direction. The reactors instantly went into emergency shutdown when the envelope field began to leak.

My destination was the pole with the blue pennant. The pole was standing at the center of the large sand square all alone. Only a few flat and unused barracks delimited the square.

I was standing at the corner of one of the buildings now, looking around. Once I touched the pole, the operation was over.

But six camouflaged suits were standing around the pole shoulder to shoulder. I could have jumped past them, but it was too easy. I knew this was a decoy. I needed to find the real trap.

I searched the buildings in the area. There was a possibility that more suits were hiding in there. But I deemed it unlikely, since they could only target me after I touched the pole. I just had to make sure not to leave new footprints in the sand. Then, I noticed it. There were no old footprints. If the suits had walked to the pole, someone must have cleared away any traces of their footsteps. But then it would've sufficed to rake it clean once. It was a puzzle, for me to solve. Why had someone taken the effort to let it appear untouched if that only made it harder to spot my footprints?

There were mines in the sand, I concluded. I couldn't miss the irregularities, which made me wonder whether I'd really spotted everything. Everything suggested that they expected me to reach the conclusion to fly across the area. So I needed to find out what they could do about an invisible flying Dragon.

I sensed no radar, heard no ultrasonic sound, saw no infrared light barriers. When invisible, people tended to forget their shadows. The camouflaged suits didn't fare any better than me there, but close to the ground the suit could project enough light to clear any shadow on the ground. That didn't work in the air.

I could ponder for days here. Instead, I sent out a nano wire.

CHAPTER SEVENTY-NINE

Fatima and her tandem partner Moses were sitting opposite me and waiting. Except for a brief military salute and an invitation to this improvised conference room in one of the barracks, neither of them had said a word so far.

Moses had short black curls, thin whiskers and laugh lines in the corners of his eyes. He appealed to me. Moses was well equipped under his skintight suit, but it seemed inappropriate for me to poach in Fatima's territory.

According to his reports, he was a very competent officer. I appreciated that he seemed to match her in the private area, too. If there was such a thing as a private area in the armored infantry.

"Okay. The idea of the linear cannons with shadow sensors was excellent. Whose idea was that?"

"Pedro's," Fatima replied. "He's very creative."

"That's good. We need creativity."

Both remained silent.

"Fatima, say something. Give me your judgments on the mission's results."

"We failed."

"Barely. On my way, your people almost got me twice, and the trap at the end was good, too. By the way, how's the team with the reactor failure doing?"

"Aside from a light burn in the back, good. Why twice?"

"When I broke through the perimeter around the monastery, one of you shot at me."

"Oh. That was recorded as a mistake."

"It wasn't. So, go on."

"Go on with what?"

"Your assessment. You failed. What was the reason? Was it your strategic judgment of the situation?"

She hesitated, so I gave the answer myself. "No. With such a large area, two encounters are a sign of a very effective coverage. If you had deployed the people tighter around this place, reinforcements would have arrived earlier at the second encounter. In exchange, my odds for slipping through your net elsewhere would've increased."

I saw her begin to relax a little. "Your individual measures were good, as well. The people had assumed well-concealed positions from which they could control large areas. They could *effectively* control the area, as the second encounter proved. I particularly liked the encircling shooting pattern. That one almost got me."

At this remark, Fatima flinched.

"Are you worried about that? I admit this exercise was *very* realistic. Your people gave me something to chew on, and under very unlucky circumstances I could have contracted an ugly injury. But that was the deal. No rules."

"No rules," Moses quietly echoed. He placed a hand on Fatima's shoulder.

"I'm *not* mad about that. It was challenging and dangerous, but it met the agreement, and your troops were good. I'm really glad to know Earth's defense is in such competent hands."

I leaned back, which presented my breasts a bit better, and watched Moses from the corner of my eyes while addressing Fatima.

"You're so good that nobody would seriously follow up on the idea of two more locations. If we opened a second training center in the USA, we could only offer the second-best training there. No. The whole world will instead send its best male and female soldiers to the Emirates—to you. And so you're already leading an entire regiment. Congratulations, *Brigadier General* Fatima saba Rashid. Congratulations, Colonel Moses Perez. The council formally approves your promotions."

"You're not mad at us?" the new general asked.

"No. Just the opposite, I'm impressed. You promised to make the operation interesting, and you kept your promise. That shows me once again that you can pull through unpleasant tasks, and that you can be trusted with the proverbial hot potato. That's important, because I'll soon have to leave for a longer journey. In the meantime, I have a few new tasks for you."

"And what would those be?" Moses asked.

I raised three fingers and tapped the first. "First, I want you to expand the unit. We—the Council, the Secretary and I—want to have at least a training and a reserve battalion. Second, I want you to identify tandem teams that are suited for special missions, let's say, for longer independent missions behind the enemy lines, without access to the line of command. Third, you shall expand your area of training to the jungle, high mountains, Antarctica, underwater, and eventually on the moon."

"On the moon?" Fatima echoed.

"You never know."

She gave her partner a brief glance. "I assume that especially the identified special mission teams should cover the entire terrain spectrum, right? We're in."

"I don't expect anything less."

Fatima winked at me. "It needn't end with the moon."

CHAPTER EIGHTY

The Pacific's dark blue water disappeared behind me, and my Taipan sailed across the Australian mainland's green coastal strip. "Woomera Base for Gold One. Ready for training operation David."

"Woomera Base. Operation David begins now."

The guard officer on duty would trigger the alarm. First, the alert pair would start, while male and female pilots dashed to their gear, cursed, put on their pilot suits, and rushed to their fighters.

If the drill worked well, it should take no more than three minutes until the entire wing was airborne.

In the meantime, the alert pair tried an initial cautious approach. That should be a safe bet. It would be two Taipans against one, two experienced combat pilots with daily practice against an occasional pilot like me.

However, nobody knew these planes as well as I did, and my *Analogy* didn't need daily exercise to perfect my pilot skills. With a little modification of my nestle field, a pull at my flight stick, two exercise-power shots from my laser cannon, I made the two defenders' computers declare themselves shot down.

That should have given my remaining opponents a warning. But they deemed themselves good and discarded their comrades' downing as bad luck.

So the remaining thirty-four planes of the Second UNAF Combat Wing *Copperheads* — the First Wing would forever remain that of Laetitia Lionheart, commander of the first Taipan

242

wing—attacked the single intruder. Thirty-four pilots were eager to show what they'd learned during the last year. Nothing and nobody should be able to withstand their super fighters.

Nothing and nobody—except for a Dragoness who, like the famous first pilot, commanded the *combat trance.*

Seventeen seconds later, it was all over, and the entire second wing had to return to the base with engines reduced to minimal power. Meanwhile, my computer hadn't recorded as much as a grazing shot. Most of them hadn't even managed to release a shot.

The debriefing would be interesting.

The meeting with Jenny was short. The training was a lot of work, especially since Zoé no longer accompanied the practical part—for reasons Jenny didn't know—but it was fun.

"The boys and girls are incredibly motivated, and they're good—well, usually," she said.

"No argument."

At the end of the short hallway, painted in plain light gray, there were two doors to the left and right. Jenny chose the left door, where I heard quiet but excited voices.

A fine swirl of omnipresent red dust followed the draft. The conversations fell mute. A single voice calmly announced, "Attention."

"Thanks, Piers," Jenny acknowledged as she let me pass and pushed the door close behind me.

Thirty-six young people in pilot suits, all taller than me, watched me with curiosity.

"You've surely recognized the Imperatrix already," Jenny said and nodded at me.

"Hello, team," I greeted my pilots. "Let me get right to the point. You didn't have a snowball's chance in hell, but for that, you sold your hide damn well."

That confused them. I didn't wait for questions. "Sit down. Then you all have a chance to see me without me having to climb a chair. I'll explain to you what just happened and why. Then we'll get to the questions."

I waited until the shuffling of feet and chair legs stopped.

"Thanks. I told your Marshal only a few days ago that I'd pay you a visit. She said that would be a good opportunity for an entirely unexpected alarm operation with an equal opponent. We talked about your training level, and I pondered how to set up my attack — without telling Jenny."

I glanced at Jenny and turned back to my pilots. "You know the results. I taught you a painful lesson. The fight was unfair from the start because no matter how good you feel at the stick, you stand no chance against a Dragoness in full command of her powers."

I gave them a moment to let this statement sink in and settle. It was important for them to incorporate this lesson for two reasons. First, they needed to realize that they weren't invincible. Second, they had to know I could beat them anytime. That was the same lesson I had just taught the armor suits. It was my way of preventing any rebellious ideas.

"There is no doubt in my mind that you are all in the same league as the best fighter pilots on this planet, who deservedly fly the best fighters on this planet. Let's start to examine your achievements."

They seemed ready to listen now. "The alert pair was airborne twenty seconds after triggering the alarm. That shows me how seriously you take this post, and I owe a pizza to one of you."

A blond head in the third row smirked. A patch on his chest showed his name.

"Olaf?"

He nodded. I'd make sure he got his pizza.

"Okay. The alert pair flew an interception maneuver by the

book and failed epically. Why?"

I waited to see if anyone would answer. No one spoke up, so I continued.

"First, it failed because it was by the book. That allowed me to plan a counterattack for it. Second, I surprised you with a quick and precise shot across a large distance."

To make sure they understood, I recapped the relevant physics. "I know you're theoretically aware of a laser's range, and you know the practical limitations—target precision and scatter by air particles. The computer can help you with the first if you can operate it quickly enough. The latter can partially be compensated by higher power input. That's what I simulated, so my first laser would've been overheated after the two shots and wasn't available during the rest of the exercise. That was a calculated risk from my side because I hadn't expected the entire remaining wing being airborne within two-and-a-half minutes. So I had to make do with only one laser for the rest of the battle."

That had to make them think again. I had so to speak fought with one hand behind my back and still finished them off.

"Okay. Your teammates had already been shot down, and you went into battle without hesitation. If you consider that you had no time for planning and conferring, your maneuver was excellent."

Some of their faces brightened up when I complimented them. "You presented me a bait, covered the bait and at the same time prepared a pincher move—where neither of you was in anyone else's line of fire at any point in time. You were entirely correct to expect my Taipan's outer shape being the disguise for a by far more powerful opponent, and attacked with full strength without holding back a reserve."

Three of them glanced at each other and nodded—probably the masterminds behind that move. "Some of you managed to serve a shot that way. When you later examine the computer logs, you'll see that you can be proud of this performance. But what impressed me most is the fact that none of you showed as much as a tremble while around you your mates were shot down. This fighting spirit makes me proud. Jenny, your folks are outstanding."

"That almost sounds as if we couldn't teach them anything more." Jenny smiled.

I smiled back. "But there is more to learn. The next stage covers maneuvers under changed gravitational and atmospheric conditions."

"How are we going to teach them that?"

"Initially, through simulations. Once the preparations are complete, you'll fly real missions to Mars or Venus from a carrier."

"To learn how to chase Jellies there?"

"No. As preparation for an extra-solar mission."

CHAPTER EIGHTY-ONE

The flight from Woomera to our island was just a hop for my Taipan. During the approach, I was still pondering the next steps for the scout mission. We still needed to fine-tune the emitters, find equipment, and localize the destination.

I parked the plane, jumped out, waved at the invisible guard, and ambled over to our communication center.

It was quiet inside, even though I sensed the presence of numerous people in the building. Didn't they have anything to discuss? How unusual!

My Companion's familiar signature was missing. He was far away, acting as a backup for Tess and her girls. I was beginning to worry that something had happened while I was away.

I entered the communication center. Amidst cheerful and expectant faces, I spotted a large cake with burning candles. My *Analogy* counted forty-seven candles for me.

Next to the door, Nanette was waiting with two glasses of sparkling wine. She gave me one and wrapped her now free arm around my neck, pulling me into a promising kiss.

"Happy birthday to you, Jo!"

That was the cue for the other people to start singing *Happy Birthday* out loud and out of tune. I spilled my sparkling when I collapsed in Nanette's arms, crying.

Rod's strong arms carried me outside to the beach and gently let me glide down to the sand. I heard Nanette chasing Rod and Reginald away with a single sharp command. Only

247

Scrubby was allowed to stay. Several times he nudged my toes with his snout.

Nanette caressed my hair. "I thought you'd be happy," she whispered. "There, there."

"I-I am happy." For a moment, I helplessly waved my arms, and Scrubby began to lick my wet face. Of all things!

But somehow, it was nice, too. He tried to be kind to me with his pure dog mind. Who was I to deny that?

I could no longer bear Nanette's worried face. "I'm overwhelmed. You know, Nanette, that's my first birthday party in twenty-nine years."

"In twenty-nine years?"

"Somehow the opportunity never came," I answered the unasked question.

"You poor thing. Okay. I understand. It blew you away." She caressed my head again. "Just stay here, and I'll get you another glass of sparkling."

"No, it's okay." I petted Scrubby and climbed to my feet again. "You managed your surprise too well. Now that I've adapted, I want to celebrate. Who knows when the next opportunity will come?"

"Oh. Why do you say that?"

"I have a feeling I'll venture on a longer journey soon."

PART EIGHT—WORRIES

CHAPTER EIGHTY-TWO

Francine diligently dug through the results of *Mischief's* last deep analysis. I briefly examined our plot and checked the program parameters for what felt like the hundredth time. We had a few minutes before the programmed transit point.

I sighed, and we looked at each other. She grinned at me, and I shrugged back. We understood each other. There was nothing left to do.

There were no complaints about the control quark emitter's fine tuning. It was too late to buy a forgotten toothbrush now. We had to make do with the available equipment. We didn't have much room left, since every available corner of the little spaceship was crammed with supplies, measuring instruments, and other necessary equipment. Even the previously spacious pilot cabin offered little elbow room. Only the bedrooms, sanitary unit, and galley were left untouched for us.

It was too late to change the crew, too. Of course, there had been discussions on who should handle such a mission. A lot of people had questioned why I had to go.

I told them I wouldn't expose anyone else to this risk because I was scientifically and technically competent. I was the only one with practical experience, thanks to my test flight. Plus, my odds of survival were better. I could keep contact with my Companion across interstellar distances and thus could report back results even if we were no longer able to return. But most of all, I wanted to go.

Rashid had pestered me about it. Reginald had pestered me. Rod and Tim had asked me about it. Even Nanette, who otherwise never interfered, had bothered to ask me about it.

One after another, different politicians had asked whether this truly was the only solution. Even the Russians and Chinese had hinted at concerns, and that was truly a breakthrough. I had an inkling though that they finally understood that I was the one safeguarding their equal chances in a rather Western-oriented environment.

In the end, no one could stop me. This was my mission. Mine — and Francine's. She refused to take no for an answer.

"I'm your pilot," she insisted. "Nobody else knows this bird like I do, and you need someone to keep her eyes open while you dig into a problem. Otherwise, I'm expendable."

She didn't voice it, but she assumed this transit would no longer be lethal, so there was a high chance that she would survive this mission. Moreover, I had to admit I was happy to have her company. That feeling was mutual.

The transit should cover about one hundred and forty light years. No matter the distance, it was the first true interstellar spaceflight in a ship that had exclusively been invented and created on Earth. Martha had finally found the far end of our last visitor's wormhole in our data, providing us with the destination system, thanks to Eduardo, who had developed a fuzzy filter algorithm that could find and compare more possible patterns with fewer specs. Rashid's tip hadn't helped us, because our data didn't reach back far enough to record the Jelly arrival in the destination system.

Of course, the destination's sun had a scientific name, but we just called it *Worries,* because the system worried us. The postulated planet would consequently be called *Trouble.* We only had to find it yet.

The computer granted us five more seconds. Francine flicked her virtual dashboard away, leaned back, and winked at me.

I winked back. Then my senses ran wild.

CHAPTER EIGHTY-THREE

The transit seemed to be infinite. When our miniverse finally spat us out, my stomach felt like it would turn inside out.

I fought that feeling down. All my senses relayed alarming signals. A ringing bell, red light, heat, the stench of sweat, dizziness . . . stop!

Francine?

She was alive and fighting her nausea. She gave me the universal *okay* signal by placing her thumb and index finger together. Good. The last I needed now was vomit drifting freely through our zero-gravity cockpit and threatening to enter our air ducts.

I turned my attention to the computer's ringing collision alert. Red was the predominant color on our screens. I flicked my dashboard up and browsed the symbols. Life support symbols showed yellow and green. I acknowledged and discarded the warning. The ships' body integrity indicator flickered yellow, so it was worsening, but I didn't immediately see a reason why.

Fusion reactors were at yellow without flickers. They weren't to blame. Nestle field and shield were red. I tapped there. Eighty percent of our control quark emitters were damaged or already burned up.

So we were racing into a foreign system at twenty percent light speed. Between us and the interstellar dust, there was just a thin layer of self-repairing nanos and molecular-reinforced steel left, and outside a patchy web instead of a shield.

Einstein's formula, $E=mc^2$, was merciless. Even a picogram of dust hitting us was hitting us with energy squaring our speed, and these 360 millijoules per particle meant pure destruction.

The computer couldn't make up its mind between the programmed deceleration and the protective envelope and tried both, which only further stressed our emitters.

I completely deactivated the nestle field and reduced the protective envelope to a small shield in flight direction. The flickering stopped; now the shield was only red. So I advised the repair nanos to repair only the forward emitters first, then coarsely patch the body damage.

The ringing ceased. For the moment, I'd bought us some time.

"Sorry. How's it looking?" Francine activated her dashboard and glanced at the screen. "No deceleration?"

"Crappy. No. But we're alive."

"We're alive." She showed her teeth. "Fortune favors the brave."

"Yes. Okay, I'll give you the summary. The transit went as planned. We exited where we wanted to, about twenty billion kilometers away from *Worries*. But the exit from transit overloaded the emitters. The computer did its best to get us through in one piece, but eighty percent of the emitters are gone."

"Oh. Beyond repair? Then we're stuck here?"

"For now, we're stuck here, yes." I didn't evade her gaze. "If we can't replace the emitters, we can't get away from here. Moreover, we have no nestle field for the drive and no complete shield. The few emitters still working are currently shielding us against the interstellar dust. The body is damaged, but still intact. Without emitters, we can't use the cake knife and can't create artificial gravity."

"Jelly crap."

"Let's look at the brighter side. We're still alive, the body is intact, and all our instruments are ready to do their tasks. We can still complete our mission."

That wasn't what Francine wanted to hear. "We have repair nanos and raw material aboard so we can do something about our situation. I don't want to rule out a return right now."

"That sounds better already. Moreover, we've got you."

I smiled. "I don't want to give you false hopes. I don't know whether we can replace eighty percent of the emitters, and most of all, I don't know whether that would help. In any case, I will only allow our nanos to work on them once I know what made them fail. I'm sure the fine tuning's okay."

"What can I do?"

"Take care of the mission. Try to find out everything about this system. Most importantly, find out if there's another Jelly ship. Once we're sure nothing can cause us harm, we apply the old grav field drive and give ourselves gravity."

"Okay, clear."

Good Francine. Like her fellow Mambas, she'd survived for years in the Cartel's grasp. If she had learned one thing there, it was patience. As long as she was alive, she wouldn't give up.

CHAPTER EIGHTY-FOUR

Francine had already brought me my third cup of coffee. Since her readings and observations hadn't yielded immediate hints on a Jelly presence — or any spacecraft — I allowed us a tenth g deceleration with the grav field generator. We'd compute later how to manage a reasonable swing-by around *Worries* that way.

"What did you find out?" she asked.

"The greater the transit distance, the greater the potential equalization upon reentry. Our travel bubble carries the space-time structure and everything belonging to it — like the solar system's gravitational effects, the entire galaxy, light, cosmic radiation, magnetism, and who knows what else — from the beginning. The space-time structure in the destination system is different, and upon re-entry, there's an equalization."

I took the cup. "Thanks. I guess that with a normal wormhole, the potential equalization happens gradually, as start and end are connected by the hole. I didn't calculate that through. With our tunnel, it happens at the end and puts significant stress on the bubble. We were very fortunate that the emitters worked long enough to get us out."

"And? Can we repair them?"

"We can. Only that's of little help for us, since they'd be exposed to the same stress on our way back. I don't know whether we'd be lucky again. We can repair the emitters and then have our nestle field and our shield back, but we won't be long-range capable that way. We need stronger emitters. I have yet to calculate how strong our emitters need to be to get us home safely."

"It doesn't seem like we're pressed for time."

"No, not right now. We won't starve yet. It all hinges on our water. If the repair takes longer, we'll have to find water. That's another job for you. I prefer to avoid landing on *Trouble* for it." I took a deep breath. "Perhaps we'll have to do it anyway."

"Why?"

"Because we must install the new emitters *outside.*"

While *Mischief* was racing further into the system with low deceleration, I continued my calculations for our emitters. Meanwhile, Francine diligently analyzed our readings.

During a rather frugal dinner, I listened to what she had to report. She showed me a map of the system.

"This system has three planets. Two of them could be habitable. The innermost planet is slightly larger than Earth and hotter. There should be plenty of water. The planet's volcanic eruptions must be quite severe. Number two is a small ice ball. I believe that if there's life on this popsicle, it can only be found inside ice caves. Quite a way farther out is the last planet, a fat gas ball."

"Does it have any moons?"

"There are a few rocks around the gas ball."

"Have a closer look at them. If I have to put *Mischief* down somewhere, I'd rather it be on a rock without atmosphere than an ice inferno or next to an active volcano."

"Sure, I'll look into it."

I tapped the screen. "Number one looks like our candidate. The volcanoes promise mainly trouble. So that's *Trouble.*"

Francine nodded. "I agree. Number two wouldn't do watery Jellies any good, would it?"

"Surely not, but we don't know how they'd live on ice

planets. Did you find any traces of left-behind Jellies?"

She quickly swallowed a bite. "I found traces of radioactive isotopes in *Trouble's* atmosphere. Our eggheads had said we would find such if the Jellies had triggered an EMP. But I couldn't find anything else. We're not close enough for camera images. If you ask me, sending a rover there will be an adventure in and of itself."

I sighed.

"It's too early to rack your brains about that, isn't it?" she asked emphatically. "I thought about this potential equalization. During your test flight, this was not a problem, right?"

"Wrong. I discovered this problem on my first test flight. That's why we wanted to improve the fine tuning. We've misinterpreted the recognized wear."

"A pity."

"Why?"

"I had thought several shorter legs might be gentler."

I pondered briefly. "This idea is worth following up. Mmm — we don't have a pinboard here."

Francine shrugged. "I'll make one on the computer. You think there's something to it?"

"Sure. Once I have a formula describing the observed effect, I'll know how it relates to distance. If it grows more than linear, your idea pays off, and that's quite likely. Ask me again in two or three weeks."

"In two weeks?"

"Yes. I'm sorry, but I don't have a solid approach yet. I must first get some basics straight. This takes me to another issue. We must be able to steer. Otherwise, we'll shoot past the target soon. I don't trust the grav field drive alone. So I'll instruct the repair nanos to reconstruct the emitters with our available resources, although I'd prefer to postpone that until I knew what kind of improvement we'll have to apply to them. Then we can erect a nestle field or a shield. Sadly, that also means we need to procure more raw material even if that means we have to pillage the torpedoes."

My pilot pressed her lips together. After a short pause, she said, "So you don't know yet how much stronger the emitters must be?"

"Well, I can estimate the required upgrade we need to get home, since we have readings on that. We must be able to send about four times as many control quarks at the same time. Of course, the quarks must be sent out with precise adjustments, and we need more variation in the tunnel field — that is, more variety in the messages that will be sent. That'll cost computing power, too, but we've got that. Both will put the emitters under more strain, though."

"Why?"

"Because it's not only emitting the quarks that strains the emitter, but their coding. It's been the same since the very first envelope field built with the Meier effect."

Francine moved a hand through her hair. "But our reactor doesn't have stress, or . . ."

"No." I watched my pilot closely. Her eyes flicked back and forth more than before, and she was breathing faster. She was stressed. Sadly, I couldn't tell her any good news yet.

"Unfortunately, I have no formula for the potential equalization yet, and no new programming for the emitters either. Plus, I don't know how the new emitters should be built to bear the additional strain."

It was probably better if I told her everything. "Honestly, I don't even know if a larger spaceship's emitters — for example, those of a Phoenix — could safely manage this balancing act."

She leaned forward in her seat. "All's fine and well, but why does our reactor work without trouble? What did you guys change?"

I paused and mused about her question. "I don't know for

sure. We never talked about it directly. Wait, we've got the specs in our database."

I searched for the data on my virtual dashboard. The computer projected a three-dimensional reactor image and highlighted the emitters.

"There are more," I noted. "Yes, sure — for the orthogonal signals. So the emitters don't have to switch back and forth. That's how it works for our nestle field, too. There are emitter groups for the different control signals."

Francine smiled. "Okay. So if we had four times as many emitters, they'd only have to accept a new adjustment every fourth time, right?"

"Not quite. The adjustment changes every time."

"But the time interval per emitter would be larger."

"Right." Her idea sadly had a catch — no, two. "For four times as many emitters, we need more resources. That's the easy part. We also need the space to mount them and the respective power and control lines. It'll require us to reconstruct the ship almost entirely."

CHAPTER EIGHTY-FIVE

I could have put it differently — we were stuck in this system. Theoretically thinking about crawling home at a twenty percent light speed wasn't worth the effort.

Of course, I wouldn't give up searching for a solution, but with the available resources, I could at best bring *Mischief* to about eighty percent of her nominal performance. For a complete overhaul, I'd need a safe wharf to work outside, plenty of raw materials and at least half a year to transform it into tool nanos in a nurturing tank.

The good news was that there existed enough raw material in this system. The bad news was that we had food reserves for only a few months, not for half a year. Even worse, some of the necessary substances were only available on *Trouble*.

We'd have to land there to get them aboard — with a spaceship with an outer hull made from nanos, which presented an irresistible bait for the strange brown pest that we expected there.

Not to mention the nanos of our protective suits and inside my body. No, these raw materials were out of our reach.

The same problem that kept us here also kept any support from Earth away from us. As long as we hadn't solved the potential equalization problem, it was irresponsible to send anyone after us.

I had to admit to myself that I couldn't solve this problem on my own. I didn't have a half-finished Meier potential equalizer to pull from an imaginary hat, and all my other Dragon skills couldn't conjure up a solution for me.

Potential equalizer? Okay, Jo.

"Please bring me a large cup of hot chocolate," I told Francine.

She nodded, unbelted herself, and cautiously pushed herself out of her seat. At only a tenth of Earth's gravity, as caused by our deceleration, any forceful move would make her hit the ceiling.

CHAPTER EIGHTY-SIX

Francine quietly watched me drinking my hot chocolate in small sips. Several times, she bit her lips.

"You can ask," I finally said.

She smiled. "I didn't want to disturb your thoughts."

"You're never a disturbance. At the moment, I'm trying to let my blocked thoughts dangle. Right now, I don't know what to do. I'm not sure if I'm just on the wrong track or if this situation is truly inescapable."

"Explain it to me again." She spread her arms. "It's not as if I have to leave urgently."

No, there she was right. I unfolded my previous considerations before her. Several times, she asked me for further details, then again for a simpler explanation. Finally, she nodded.

"Let me describe it in my own words," she began. "Our *Mischief* is severely damaged, despite the improved fine tuning. The primary cause is the difference between the space-time potentials at entry and at exit that hits us like a hammer upon exit. If our repair nanos do their job with all the available resources we have left, we can run at eighty percent capacity. That's enough to slow down or speed up, and that's also enough to take us into the tunnel. However, when we arrive home, the potential's shock will take us apart. Correct?"

"Correct."

"Okay. We can't rebuild our little one. We have no raw materials for that. Even if we wanted to rebuild *Mischief*, we'd have to land somewhere in this system and do repairs outside. That could be dangerous. Why do we have to land, again?"

"So that I can work at the outer hull."

Francine nodded. "What exactly do you expect to gain from working dirtside? Gravity? Or breathable air? What if you face a stormy, perhaps even damaging atmosphere instead? In that case, you'd have to shield yourself. Do you have enough power to do that?"

I stared at her.

My pilot nodded again. "That doesn't help us at all, right? We'd have to find a protected place, and that won't be easy. But if we could protect the ship from the outside with our own devices, we wouldn't have to land, correct?"

"Correct."

"Couldn't we reassign an emergency cocoon to do that?"

"Right. We'll just wrap parts of the hull in a cocoon, and I can do my work inside it. Francine, you're a genius."

She raised her eyebrows in amusement. "No way. That's your job. I'm just practical."

"I tell you what's truly practical. Angry April once said to Zoe — *I'm a down-to-earth girl. I need something to throw a hand grenade at.* That's practical."

Francine pretended to throw something, and I ducked away. Then she made a stern face. "So we could rebuild without landing, only we don't have the raw materials."

"And we don't have the blueprints."

"You know, Jo, for this single tunnel transit, I wouldn't care much how clean you calculated your formulas. It only has to work once — like April's grenade, only not as destructive. But that's the problem."

She raised her hands and began to enumerate with her fingers. "We can't cover the distance in one leg because that will tear us apart. We can't do it in several small steps, as the emitters suffer a little damage each time, and we can't be sure if they'll hold till the end.

"If they fail, we're stuck *somewhere* and perhaps worse off than now. We could hop from star to star, but if our stopover has no planets with raw materials, we're fucked. We can't risk searching for raw materials here because we could be infected by the brown stuff. We're better off destroying ourselves before we carry that pest home."

I nodded. On this first mission, there could be no contamination risk — on no account.

"I don't understand one thing, though. Why do we have to take this potential equalization in one big hit? Why not emerge very slowly?"

"No," I said spontaneously. Then I frowned. *Why not, actually?*

CHAPTER EIGHTY-SEVEN

No, we couldn't emerge slowly. There was indeed a finite time interval greater than zero, during which we performed the transition into transit and out of transit. Unfortunately, this timespan couldn't be controlled with anything we had on the ship.

"It's like a water droplet detaching from a tap. The hanging drop can form slowly, but at some point, it must detach, and from that moment on, the tunnel field is established. In reverse, the same applies. The drop hits the water's surface and merges with the rest. Splash."

"Splash," Francine echoed. "I understand. So, we're accelerating like a falling drop. Does it have to be like that? Or could we merge with the water as gently as we detached before?"

I made a face. "That's how it is with comparisons. No, as far as my formulas apply, we're not accelerating. The speed in transit depends on how well the bubble's shielded. Again, the quality of the shielding is owed to the fine tuning. We also don't detach gently but tear ourselves off by brute force. We slip through the transit and penetrate normal Einstein Space just as brutally. It's not quite as violent as a big wormhole, but it is micro-invasive."

Francine leaned forward. "No. There's still something wrong. What happens when we do a short transit? We're just as fast, we must tear us away and splash back, but the wear fails to appear."

"That's the potential equalization."

"Yes, you explained that. But the equalization then is independent of the penetration, isn't it? Why do we have to postpone it until the last moment? Don't we know the space-time structure at our destination?"

I stared at her while the wheels in my head started to click. But she wasn't done yet.

"I paid attention. You said something about gravitational effects, magnetism, cosmic radiation — um — light, and a big unknown. I don't care for the big unknown, but we should be able to calculate the gravitational situation in our destination system, and if we can create artificial gravity in our cabin, we can do it for the entire bubble?"

"But not adapted . . ." Before I could finish, she continued thinking out loud.

"During transit, I don't give a damn about artificial gravity. At that moment I don't know where's up and down anyway." Expectantly, or even challengingly, she stared at me. "Well?"

My *Analogy* was already helping me assemble the respective formula set. Of course I'd have to simulate it, and to be sure, test it with a short transit, but basically, I already knew the result.

"What's up? Why are you grinning?"

I winked at my teammate. "Congratulations. You've just invented the *Besson compensator*. Welcome in the egghead ranks."

Still grinning, I unbelted myself and swung toward the galley, leaving her high-volume protest behind me. I needed coffee. Later, I explained how a scientific breakthrough could be named after an individual to her by telling her a story about copulating elementary parts.

CHAPTER EIGHTY-EIGHT

There wasn't much left to do for us but stare at the last deep analysis computer report or the countdown together. Francine reached out a hand, and I took it and briefly squeezed it.

It has to work, I told myself. *It has to!*

We had done two test transits. Twice, we risked straining our emitters further, which would have ultimately deprived us of any possibility of return.

The first time, we jumped a few light seconds without compensation. The emitters hadn't complained. They just swallowed minor potential differences.

The second time, the emitters were permitted to compensate during transit. The result had surprised us. Not only had the transition been significantly gentler, but the transit itself had required less energy because the continuous equalization made maintaining the bubble easier.

We could confidently look ahead to the transit home.

If the Meier gravtunnel would work with low-performance emitters . . .

If the Besson compensator could make up for the missing emitters . . .

If I had correctly calculated the space-time structure at our destination and matched it with our readings from home . . .

If the Besson compensator could master the respective potential equalization upon reentry . . .

If the effects we knew or expected were truly the decisive ones . . .

If the computer reconfigured the emitters to a forward-facing shield upon reentry as planned . . .

If I didn't introduce an error during the numerous programming changes, which had played hide and seek during the following simulations . . .

If Murphy's Law would leave us alone this one time . . .

Three.

I let Francine's hand go.

Two.

I took a deep breath.

One.

Achrotzyber!

Zero.

CHAPTER EIGHTY-NINE

The dizziness faded. A little hesitant, I opened my eyes. I wasn't sure if I wanted to know what was going on around me.

No alarm signals.

No flashing red lights on my dashboard.

Sporadically, I saw amber signals—for the body integrity, the forward shield status, the artificial gravity, for our position with our own sun in the center of the plot and on the forward-facing screen—and a single red signal for our central weapons bay, which could no longer be ready due to a lack of emitters. The message was irrelevant, but the computer did its duty.

My pilot feebly waved.

"Better," she said. "Much better."

"It rocked, didn't it? It worked this time."

"Sufficiently." She glanced at her controls. "Amber only?"

"Amber only. Do a deep analysis."

She rubbed her temples. "Only a few emitters show minor signs of wear—about three percent instead of eighty. We could start again."

"We might have to do that soon."

"Why?" She sat up abruptly and stared at me.

I spread my arms apologetically. "I'm an idiot. I had completely forgotten to notify my Companion. If we failed this transition, we'd botch the mission."

Francine frowned. "I see. You want to return, so that you can mentally feed him our readings and problems from the distant system, instead of simply sending it to Earth by radio from here."

"Yes, of course."

Her eyes widened.

"No, seriously, of course not," I corrected. "I only said I had forgotten. Right before the transit, I thought of him and involuntarily transmitted. Just one impulse."

"Yes, so? If he received the impulse, we now know it works even when you're in a different system. Did you ask him if he got it yet?"

"No. I know it works because I sensed his echo."

"Fine. So, let's get that nestle field ready and slip down to Earth?" She started the deep analysis and instructed the computer to give us artificial gravity.

"I didn't sense his echo alone, Francine."

Her fingertips paused over the virtual dashboard. "What does that mean?"

"In the *Worries* system, there are Dragons."

To be continued . . .

You may also enjoy the following from eXtasy Books Inc:

LOSER
Lioness' Legacy I
Valerie J. Long
October 24, 2012

Excerpt

The building rose high above the rocky cliff, at the foot of which the waves' anger broke. Tiny oriels and slender turrets should have made it look like a fairy castle, futile in this harsh environment. Storm and rain battered against it — in any case, the weather was too uninviting for a longer outdoor stay, so the guards had retreated to the warm inside.

For observation purposes, they still had weatherproof cameras aiming at the sea around the cliff. There was a chance that a smaller boat wouldn't be recognizable in rain and spray, but who'd take the risk to be smashed to pieces against these cliffs in such a small vessel?

I didn't. I had studied the currents and decided to cover the last kilometers swimming. Even if the small waterproof backpack looked like a hump, I was confident I'd reach the cliff base undetected. My black hair surely wouldn't show in the dark, either.

I was also confident I'd reach the cliffs unhurt. Focused and in tune with the waves' rhythm, I accelerated for the last leg, took another deep breath and then dived down.

Sight under water wasn't much better than at the surface, and the current no weaker, but at least there was no spray. Yes, I was on the right course. A few more strokes, a few firm flaps with my fins—I shot from the water like a penguin and came down precisely on the large rock flank I had aimed for. With effort, my hands found hold in cracks across the slippery surface, where they stirred up the hermit crabs, hidden from seagulls and wash. My fin-equipped legs hung free in the air, and my knees painfully hit the rock. *Ouch. Accomplished!*

With several pull-ups, I conquered the rock top before the waves, reaching after me, could tear me off the cliff. The little claws I had mounted to the sides of the fins didn't help me much.

On top of the rock, I was safe from the waves. In exchange, I now was fully exposed to the storm. I patiently put up with it, as it was my ally. Surveillance cameras didn't suddenly lean forward to peek over the edge of the cliff, and I didn't want to be seen. So I now also undressed from the olive-green-speckled wetsuit that I wore over my sand-colored microfiber bodysuit.

Diver suit and fins had to remain behind, stuck into a crack, when I tackled the rocky wall. In exchange, my backpack provided me with thin rubber gloves and socks that should compensate for the inevitable wetness. I surely didn't need to try talcum here!

I'm sure the ascent would have been a true challenge even for an experienced free climber. The rocky wall was weathered and cracked, but—due to the rain—wet all over and mostly slippery. It took me a long time to reach the cliff top, and I felt quite exhausted—most of all mentally, because the fear of dropping down on the ragged rocks had been the worst of the entire climb. Thus, I was threefold soaking wet—first from the rain, second from the strain, third from my cold sweat.

Be calm, girl, you're not inside yet.

My next target was a small window on the third floor of the tower to my left, for three reasons. First, the left tower with its regular grooves and the arrester was easier to climb than the already evenly plastered right one. Second, the window served the painters inside as smoker's corner. With his third beer, the senior journeyman had given away that the lock and alarm for this window currently didn't work, but that was no issue—hardly anyone could get through such a small window. A dainty girl like me, perhaps, but only if I could master the cliff, and who could do that, after all?

Only someone who was small and still strong could do that. Someone who could swim several kilometers and still could climb thereafter, or could run a marathon. Someone who could regularly finish an Ironman among the top ten. Like myself.

About the Author

I am Valerie J. Long, born in 1963. I live and work in Germany as an IT project manager. I like role playing games, and I like putting my ideas on paper. I like all kinds of Science Fiction and Fantasy, I like music, and I like making you bite your nails off.